CHRISTMAS MOON OVER HOLLY POINTE

CINDY KIRK

D1526911

WAVERLY
HOUSE

ISBN: 9798858762478

CHAPTER ONE

Melinda Kelly took a long sip of her latte and cast a lazy glance around the busy airport. People scurried about JFK like Christmas mice with much to do before the big day.

Not Melinda. She had only one thing to accomplish, and that was to get on a plane to Mexico scheduled to leave in less than an hour. Once she ticked that off her list, the only thing on her agenda was to chill.

This would be the first Christmas season that she wouldn't spend in her hometown of Holly Pointe, Vermont.

According to many, Holly Pointe, the Capital of Christmas Kindness, was *the* place to be for the holidays. The events! The traditions! The influx of tourists!

This year, Melinda had impulsively decided to trade snow for sand and spend her holiday in sunny Mexico. Though she felt really good about her decision, her friends were not fully convinced it was the right choice.

While they could understand the lure of the beach, they had difficulty believing anyone would willingly choose to spend the holidays alone. Considering most of them were coupled up and that even her mother and brother planned on bringing their new partners to Christmas dinner, Mel knew she'd be just as "alone" if she stayed home.

At least this way, she'd have margaritas and the beach.

She took another long sip of the caramel latte and considered the first thing she would do when she arrived at the resort. Change into her bikini and head for the pool? Take a nap so she would be ready for a night of partying?

A short nap, she decided, *at* the pool. This morning, she'd had to get up super early to catch the bus that had brought her from Vermont to New York City. Excitement might have carried her this far, but she wanted to be fresh for—

The sound of a male voice raised in anger had Melinda turning.

A tall man dressed in Bermuda shorts and a brightly patterned shirt pointed a finger at the gate agent. "Need I remind you again that I'm a Platinum member? You will give me an upgrade, and you'll do it now."

Even though Melinda wasn't seated close, his voice reached to the end of the gate area.

"Someone isn't happy." A man who looked to be about her age, with dark brown hair and blue eyes, dropped into the seat beside her, setting his leather carry-on on the floor by his feet.

"Platinum members get to board first, and some of them treat the gate agents horribly," Melinda responded dryly.

The stranger chuckled. "These frequent-flyer perks are really getting out of control."

Melinda smiled and might have said more, but her phone pinged.

Pulling it from her bag, she glanced down at the screen. Her heart gave a solid thump against her rib cage.

"At least his flight seems to be on time." Melinda resisted the urge to sigh. "Mine is delayed thirty minutes."

Barely a blip, Melinda assured herself. There would still be plenty of time for fun in the sun once she arrived.

"Mine is delayed, too." He offered a good-natured smile, appearing not at all upset by the delay.

Another ping from her phone.

And, at the same time, a ping from his.

Melinda stared down at her phone, then up at the screen at the departure gate. Her flight was no longer delayed. It was canceled.

Even though she didn't comment on the cancellation, Mr. Blue Eyes spoke to her—or perhaps to himself—in the same affable tone. "Computer system malfunction."

"What?"

"You were wondering why the cancellation."

"How did you know?"

"I checked the airline app."

Her brows slammed together. "When?"

"While you were staring at your phone."

"It'll be okay." Melinda had spoken aloud, but she wasn't sure if she'd been talking to herself or to him. "I'll get a later flight."

Melinda glanced at the long line already forming in front of the lone gate agent and knew that the airline's customer service lines would be equally impossible.

Another notice popped up on her phone. Once again, Melinda found herself staring. "I've been automatically rebooked for the twenty-ninth."

"Same here." He tossed the words out there as if they were of no consequence.

Melinda felt her control slip. "They can't do this."

"It appears it's a done deal. No Christmas in Mexico for me this year." Mr. Blue Eyes sounded pleased by the thought.

She turned to him. "The twenty-ninth is more than a week away."

4 | CINDY KIRK

"If the malfunction is systemwide, it will take time to correct."
He shrugged. "At this time of year, seats on all the airlines are usually fully booked until after the holidays."

"You don't seem upset." She found herself irritated by his nonchalance. Which made absolutely no sense. What did she care about his outlook?

"I wasn't eager to spend my Christmas with palm trees."

"Well, I was." She cleared her throat and rephrased. "I am."

Unable to rebook a flight earlier than the twenty-ninth online, Melinda resorted to her least favorite option—calling the airline directly, where she found herself placed automatically on hold.

"Drat," she muttered.

"Problem?"

"I'm on hold."

"Sucks."

He'd pulled out his laptop, and his fingers flew across the keyboard. Whatever he was doing, he was not rebooking a flight.

Melinda considered herself to be a positive, optimistic person. But she was beginning to have a sinking feeling that her anticipated adventure wasn't headed for a happy ending.

Once he finished typing, he shifted to face her. "What resort were you headed to?"

She told him.

"Me, too." He extended a hand. "Jack McPherson."

She gave his hand a quick shake. "Melinda Kelly."

"I'm not leaving this spot until you get me on another flight. Today." The loud voice cut through the buzz of conversation in the waiting area. "In first class."

They both turned toward the counter.

Same guy.

"I'm sorry, sir, but as we announced, all flights to that destination are grounded until we—"

"If you're not going to do your job, get me a supervisor."

"Sir, I'm trying—"

"Young lady, I've had enough of your excuses and your incompetence." His voice sliced the air like a whip. "Do you know who I am?"

"If I was dressed like that, I wouldn't want anyone to know who I was," a lady across the aisle from Melinda said loudly.

Laughter rippled around the seating area.

The man didn't appear to notice. He'd become a runaway locomotive, spewing venom as he rolled down the tracks, determined to flatten anything—and anyone—in his path.

Melinda had a brother, so she was no stranger to foul language. Still, this man's words had her widening her eyes.

"He shouldn't be allowed to speak to the gate agent like that." Melinda nearly got up to see if she could help. The fear of making the situation more difficult for the clerk had her hesitating.

"No," Jack agreed, "he shouldn't. And he won't be for much longer. Appears the cavalry has arrived."

Two airport security officers now flanked the man. Melinda couldn't hear what was being said, but the man jerked his arm away when one of the officers tried to take it.

After a tense silence, the man stalked off, his face red, his expression thunderous. A woman Melinda hadn't noticed before —his wife?—offered the gate agent an apologetic smile before hurrying after him.

"I don't know why he had to act that way." Melinda shook her head. "We're all upset. Why be nasty?"

"I've seen his type." Jack pulled a bottle of water from his carry-on and took a drink. "Entitled. Used to ordering people around. It creates an expectation."

"Didn't work for him this time."

"No, it didn't." Jack's lips curved as he took another sip.

Melinda pushed to her feet. She might as well get in line to talk to somebody. Sitting on hold was certainly getting her nowhere. Neither was chatting with some handsome guy she'd never see again after today.

"I wouldn't bother." As if he had read her mind, he gestured carelessly with one hand toward the line that now extended to the far end of the gate and was growing longer by the second. "If you want to get to Mexico, rebooking online is definitely the way to go."

"I've tried that. It won't let me rebook before the twenty-ninth." Despite her best efforts to control it, Mel heard her voice rise. She was normally unflappable, and it struck her just how much she'd been looking forward to sun and sand for Christmas. "What are you going to do?"

He considered her question for a moment. "I'm thinking I'll get a car and head to the White Mountains."

"Do you live in New Hampshire?"

"I live here in the city. My family lives in New Hampshire. In Timberhaven."

Melinda had been to the town that sat at the edge of the White Mountains numerous times. "I'm not too far from there, in Holly Pointe, Vermont."

Jack didn't immediately respond, his gaze once again riveted on his laptop. He grinned. "Got it."

She inhaled sharply and glanced at her phone. Still on hold. "You got an earlier flight?"

"No. I snagged a rental car. I suggest you do the same. What inventory they have won't last long."

Melinda realized he was right. If she got a car, at least she'd have a way to get back home without the hassle of the bus or the expense of an Uber. She preferred not to call her family. Neither her mother nor her brother had time to waste a day picking her up and taking her back to Holly Pointe.

They would if she asked, of course, but it would mess with their schedules big-time.

The first rental car sites she tried took forever to load, likely inundated with requests. She slanted a sideways glance at Jack, who appeared to be responding to emails and texts, his brows pulled together in concentration.

Melinda came up empty at several rental agencies. It wasn't fair, she thought as she struck out on yet another site. She was the one who needed a rental car, not Jack. He lived here in the city. He could take the subway or an Uber and be home in less than an hour.

Just when she was about to give up, she snagged a full-size SUV. More vehicle than she needed, but it would get her home.

Once she received the confirmation, she looked up, a smile of triumph on her lips. "I got one."

"Congratulations."

"Thank you." She pushed to her feet. "Have a Merry Christmas."

"Same to you. Safe travels."

The hold music still played softly from the speaker on her phone.

Jack gestured to the phone. "You realize remaining on hold is pointless."

"You're right." Though his matter-of-fact, almost cheery acceptance of the flight cancellation grated, Melinda accepted that there was no point in waiting for a customer service person to tell her what she already knew. Clicking off the call, she dropped the phone into her purse.

He rose and picked up his bag, then surprised her by falling into step beside her.

"Are you following me?" she teased, feeling oddly light-hearted. Or as lighthearted as a woman could feel after watching her vacation plans go up in smoke.

He grinned. "If you're headed to the car rental area, then the answer is yes."

They took the steps instead of the escalator, which was jammed with people. Melinda only hoped all these people weren't planning to pick up rental cars.

The flight monitors they strode by showed rows and rows of canceled flights.

At this point, the best she could hope for was an uneventful drive back to Vermont.

The ringing of Jack's phone had her shifting a glance sideways before refocusing ahead. Still, since they were nearly shoulder to shoulder because of the crowd, she couldn't help overhearing his call.

"Mom. You got my text. That's right. I'm not going to make it after all." He listened intently for a long moment, a muscle in his jaw jumping. "I planned to come. I was at the gate when my flight was canceled." His expression turned to granite. "There are no flights out of JFK to Mexico on any airline, and there's no way I'd find a flight out of any of the nearby airports either, since it's Christmas. They rebooked me on a flight on the twenty-ninth. Yes, I know that means I'll miss the wedding. Look, tell Sam I tried, but I can't make it. Give him," he hesitated for half a second, "and Natalie my best."

After listening for several more seconds, he expelled a breath. "If you don't believe me, Google 'computer meltdown' at JFK or something like that. You'll see for yourself. Have a Merry Christmas, if I don't speak with you before then."

Christmas was a week away. Surely, he would speak with his family before then.

Or—she looked at his stony expression—maybe not.

He said nothing for several seconds as the two of them continued to ride the momentum of the crowd, then he muttered, "At least that's over with."

"Problem?" she asked.

"Not anymore. It's all downhill from here." He smiled. "Tell me, why Mexico for Christmas?"

It appeared that whatever was going on between him and his family had been resolved, and he was now ready for conversation.

"I was in the mood for something different this year." She ignored the pang in the area of her heart over the trip that was not meant to be. "Don't get me wrong, Vermont is lovely this time of year…if you like unending cold and snow."

"Sorry. Not buying it."

Melinda pulled her brows together. "Buying what?"

"You seriously expect me to believe you live in Vermont and aren't a fan of winter weather?"

"Most of the time, I like it," she admitted. "This year, I wanted something different. I wanted to walk at the edge of the water and feel sand squishing between my toes. I wanted to lie on the beach with the sun hot against my skin. Instead of hot cocoa, I wanted margaritas."

Jack shook his head. "I can't imagine Christmas without snow."

"Then why were you going to Mexico?"

"Family wedding." His expression remained carefully neutral. "Kind of a command performance."

"Who's getting married?"

"My brother."

"I have a brother." Melinda inclined her head as they continued to walk. "Missing my brother's wedding would be difficult for me."

Based on the one-sided conversation she'd overheard with his mother, Jack didn't seem upset about missing his brother's wedding. Though perhaps this blasé demeanor was simply how he rolled.

"I booked the flight and packed my bags. I was ready to go. Appears it wasn't meant to be."

"Will your brother be upset when he learns you can't make it?" Melinda regretted asking the question the moment it left her lips. His family relationships were not her concern, and being a no-show was out of his control. He was as much a victim of the computer malfunction as she was. "Sorry. Don't answer that."

"Sam will get over it." Jack waved a dismissive hand, then changed the subject. "Do you often go somewhere warm for the holidays?"

She didn't have a chance to answer, because the rental car counters came into view.

"Which company?" she asked Jack.

When he told her, she smiled. "Same here."

"Look at all the people." Melinda took her place in the endless line with Jack beside her.

Another couple immediately stepped into line behind them.

The young man in front of them was a real cutie, in shorts and graphic tee, his curly hair pulled back in a man bun.

His clothing, as well as his sandals, told Melinda he'd also had a tropical destination.

"Where were you headed?" Melinda would have guessed him to be in his early twenties, though she knew he had to be at least twenty-five to rent a car.

"St. Johns." He offered a rueful smile. "How 'bout you guys?"

"Mexico." She expelled a sigh, then smiled. "I'm just thankful I was able to book a car before they were all gone."

Jack was back on his phone. His entire focus remained on the screen as the line inched forward.

Melinda passed the long wait chatting with the guy—Drew—who she learned was a graduate student at NYU.

While they talked, she tried to ignore the whining of the woman behind her as she complained to her partner, "This wasn't what I had planned."

Join the club, lady.

Melinda asked Drew, "If you live in the city, why do you need a rental car?"

"Normally, I go home to Trenton over the holidays. This year, my roommates and I rented a condo in St. John's." Drew grinned, showing a large space between his front teeth. "My buddies are already there. It's either head to Trenton to celebrate the holidays with the fam or stay in my empty apartment and celebrate alone."

Melinda was precluded from responding when the man behind the counter motioned Drew forward.

After checking Drew's reservation, the man spoke in a loud voice intended to reach to the back of the line. "I'm sorry, ladies and gentlemen, but if you're in line to pick up a car, this gentleman has gotten our last vehicle."

A loud rumble of voices sounded from behind her.

Slipping around Jack, Melinda stepped to the counter. She held up her phone. "I have a confirmed reservation."

The rental agent pushed up black glasses that kept slipping down his nose. "I'm sorry. We overbooked. I'd venture to say most of those in this line have a confirmed reservation."

Melinda could have pressed—would have—if she'd thought there was a chance that it would get her a car. But it was obvious there were no cars to be had.

Turning to leave, she paused when she overheard the conversation between Jack and Drew.

"I'll give you a hundred dollars if you give me your reservation," Jack offered, then slanted a glance at the rental agent.

The man shrugged and pushed up his glasses. "Doesn't matter to me who gets the vehicle."

"I'd like to help you out." Drew shook his head. "But driving is my fastest way home."

"The train will get you to Trenton in about ninety minutes."

The comment told Melinda that Jack hadn't been as focused on his phone as he'd appeared.

Drew gave a reluctant nod. "Yeah, but it can sometimes be a hassle."

Though Jack nodded in agreement, something told Melinda he wasn't the type to give up easily.

Jack pulled out a money clip and slipped out five crisp one-hundred-dollar bills. "Is five hundred dollars extra in your pocket worth the hassle?"

CHAPTER TWO

Drew's eyes widened. His gaze lifted from the cash to Jack's face. "Are you serious?"

"I want the vehicle."

A smile stole across Drew's face as he plucked the bills from Jack's fingers. "It's yours."

Drew turned to the rental agent. "He can have the car."

The agent grinned. "Smart move, my man."

When Jack stepped to the counter to give the rental agent his identification, Melinda touched Drew's arm as he turned to stride off.

"You didn't have to give him your car."

Drew merely chuckled and waved the bills in the air. "Have a great Christmas. I know I sure will."

The people in the line that had stretched and curved scattered to the other rental car lines now that a sign that said No Cars Available sat on the counter.

Stepping off to an area that wasn't quite so noisy, Melinda called the resort. Get this out of the way, she told herself, then tackle how to get home.

The cheery voice that answered had her hoping that somehow, she could still salvage her trip. Being there over New Year's Eve would be fun. Almost as much fun as being there for Christmas.

"This is Traci. How may I help you today?"

"Hi, Traci. This is Melinda Kelly. I have a reservation starting today."

"Of course, Ms. Kelly. We're looking forward to your arrival. Are you at the airport?"

"Not the one you're thinking of." Melinda smiled ruefully. "I'm stuck at JFK in New York City. Apparently, there is some kind of computer malfunction, and half the planes are grounded. I'm not going to be able to get there today after all."

"I'm sorry to hear that. But absolutely no worries. I can move your arrival to tomorrow and—"

"That's the thing. The airline is saying they can't rebook me until the twenty-ninth." Melinda resisted the urge to cross her fingers. "I was wondering if you could change my reservation to start then for the same number of days, just shifting the arrival and departure times."

There was a long pause on the other end of the line. "Oh, Ms. Kelly, I'd love to help you, but unfortunately we're fully booked well into January."

"You don't have anything? Not even if I pay for an upgrade?"

An upgrade would wipe out her savings, but she had really been looking forward to this trip—she needed this trip—and she wasn't willing to let it slip through her fingers.

"Let me see what I can do. Please hold."

Music filled her ear, and this time Melinda didn't cross just her fingers, but her toes as well.

"Thank you for holding."

"Did you find something for me?"

Out of the corner of her eye, she saw Jack coming toward her, but she focused on the call.

"I'm so sorry. As I stated previously, we are fully booked. However, I do have some excellent news."

"What kind of excellent news?"

"I was able to refund the money you put down, and you will not incur any additional charges for the late cancellation."

Melinda hadn't thought beyond trying to get her reservation pushed back. If she had lost her deposit and had had to pay a penalty as well…

Melinda shut her eyes for a second. She didn't even want to think about the financial hit she'd have taken.

"You okay?" Jack asked at the same time she heard Traci say, "Ms. Kelly, are you still there?"

Her eyes flew open. "Thank you, Traci. I appreciate the extra effort. Perhaps next year I'll be able to get there for Christmas."

"I'm happy I could be of assistance." The warmth in Traci's voice had Melinda wondering if the woman had heard the disappointment in her own. "I wish I could have done more."

"You were wonderful. Thanks so much." Melinda swallowed past the sudden lump in her throat. "Happy holidays."

"To you as well."

Melinda clicked off, then lowered the phone and turned to Jack. "Congrats on snagging the last car."

Concern filled his blue eyes. "Is everything okay?"

His gaze dropped to the phone she still clutched tightly.

"Yes, well…" She slipped the phone back into her bag and cleared her throat. "The bad news is the resort is booked well into January, so they can't push back my reservation. The good news is I get my deposit back, and they won't charge me a late-cancellation penalty."

"What are you going to do now?"

"You mean after I pick up the bag I checked?"

He nodded.

"I guess I'll find a place to stay in the city until I can get a bus back to Burlington tomorrow." Melinda thought of her friend Faith, who lived with her husband in the city.

Faith would welcome her with open arms, even though now wouldn't be a good time for visitors. Faith was pregnant and due any day. Gramma Ginny, who was there to watch the twin girls once Faith and Graham went to the hospital, likely occupied the spare bedroom.

Though Faith and Graham would happily make room, Melinda wouldn't impose on their hospitality.

Melinda recalled how excited she'd been when she'd rolled out of bed at oh dark thirty to catch the bus to the city. Another bus ride so soon had definitely not been part of her plans.

"You don't have family who could come and get you?"

Melinda shook her head. There was no one to take her mother's place at the diner, and her brother was in the middle of a lucrative construction job with a tight deadline.

"I'll take you to Holly Pointe," Jack offered.

"Did I hear you say Holly Pointe?"

Melinda and Jack turned as one. For a single second, the identities of the man and woman standing there didn't register. Then she realized they were the couple who had stood behind them in the car rental line.

The woman, who looked to be in her late forties, wore an anxious expression and a summer dress the color of sunflowers.

The man with her said, "Lani, you can't just ask—"

She gave her head a warning shake to cut him off and stepped closer to Jack.

"Please." The brunette's gaze remained fixed firmly on Jack. "Bill and I were headed to Mexico to celebrate our twenty-fifth wedding anniversary tonight. Obviously, that's not happening now. But if you could help us get back to Walker—that's where we live in New Hampshire—we'd both be so grateful. While it's a little out of the way to Holly Pointe, it's not that far."

She paused to take a breath, but when Jack opened his mouth, she continued before he could speak. "This way, at least, we'll be able to celebrate at home, instead of simply grabbing hoagies at the airport and waiting for the next bus in the morning."

"That would be a horrible way to celebrate." Melinda laughed lightly, acutely aware that if she didn't accept Jack's offer of a ride, that's exactly how her evening would go.

"See?" Lani flashed Melinda a smile. "Your girlfriend understands."

"I'm not his girl—" Melinda began.

"Bill and I wouldn't be any trouble, would we, honey?" Lani continued to push, her eyes pleading with Jack to agree to her request.

"No trouble at all." Bill glanced at his wife, and his expression softened. "It'd mean a lot to both of us."

To Melinda's surprise, Jack turned to her. "What do you say?"

The smile Jack flashed her was so enticing, she almost said yes before she realized she wasn't certain she understood the question.

Was he asking if she would accept a ride from him? Or if she thought he should take Lani and Bill to Walker?

"We'd be happy to pay for the gas," Bill said, as if thinking that would make their request more attractive.

"With you two living in Holly Pointe, Walker isn't that much out of the way," Lani reiterated. "Please, please help us get home. I really don't want to celebrate our anniversary in the airport. You're our only hope."

Only hope was stretching credulity. They'd gotten here, Melinda thought, and likely could figure out a way to get back to Walker. Same as she could manage to find her own way home. Though, as with them, having Jack drop her off would be much simpler.

"The reservation is for an economy car, so it'll be tight quarters." Jack smiled. "But, sure, I'll take you. The way I see it, the more the merrier."

"I told Bill I thought you were an okay guy." Lani smiled at Jack. "He thought buying off the kid was a jerk thing to do, but I said, 'Hey, it's the way of the world. Money talks.'"

Bill's face turned beet red.

Jack stared at the woman, two lines forming between his brows.

Melinda leaned close and whispered in his ear, "I think she meant it as a compliment."

Jack didn't attempt to explain himself or the situation with Drew. Instead, he simply began to walk. When he did, Melinda fell into step beside him. Lani and Bill hurried after them.

Even after they reached their flight's baggage carousel, grabbed their checked luggage and boarded the train that would take them to where the rental car was parked, Melinda still found herself waging an internal debate. Should she accept his offer of a ride or not?

"What's the matter?" Jack asked her in a low voice.

He could have spoken in a normal tone. Lani and Bill were paying no attention to them. They were focused on contacting the resort and canceling their reservation.

"I'm not sure getting into a car with a stranger is wise," Melinda told him.

"You won't be getting into a car with *a* stranger." He flashed a smile. "You'll be getting into a car with *three* strangers. Though something tells me that we'll both know Bill and Lani—especially Lani—really well by the time we drop them off."

By the time we *drop them off.*

He made it sound as if Melinda going along was a fait accompli.

Melinda's thoughts raced. She loved listening to true-crime podcasts, and so many of them started with a woman agreeing to do something her gut had no doubt said was dangerous.

The strange thing was, Melinda's gut was telling her to accept the ride. After a few seconds, she nodded. "I'll go with you. Just assure me that you're not a serial killer."

"If I had to guess, I'd say Lani is the one you have to worry about." Jack laughed. "The woman is intense."

Melinda smiled and lifted her phone. "Smile."

She texted the pic to her friends Lucy and Kate in Holly Pointe, along with a brief explanation of her plans and that, once in the car, she would activate Share ETA in the Maps app on her iPhone for them.

Lucy's response came instantly. *Nonononono. I will come and get you.*

The ding from Kate's response arrived a second later. *Do NOT get into a car with a stranger!!!!*

Melinda's heart warmed at their concern, but if she'd thought they could easily leave what they were doing to retrieve her, she would have asked.

An older couple who were also headed to Mexico is coming with us. We'll drop them off in Walker, then head to Holly Pointe. I'll send you a pic of the rental vehicle and the license plate once we get it.

After getting off the AirTrain at the Federal Circle station, they soon reached the rental lot. The economy car looked even smaller than Melinda had expected.

Jack studied the vehicle with a critical eye, then shrugged. "At least it's got a luggage rack on top."

Melinda took pictures of the car and its license plate. She was texting the pics to her friends, along with Jack's name and Timberhaven connection, when Lani asked, "What are you doing?" She stepped so close that Melinda found herself backing up.

She kept the explanation simple. "My friends Lucy and Kate asked for a pic of the car that will be bringing me home."

"Your friends need to get a life." Lani laughed and shook her head.

"Lani." Bill shot his wife a warning glance, then smiled at

Melinda. "That sounds like something our daughter-in-law would ask our son to do."

Jack's lips curved as he, with Bill's help, hefted bags into the tiny trunk and onto the top of the small car.

"We really appreciate the ride," Melinda heard Bill say.

"Glad to help out," Jack told him.

"Be careful with my bags," Lani called out, her voice rising.

Melinda had been trying to think of who Lani reminded her of, and it suddenly hit her—Lucy's mother, Paula Franks. Paula didn't handle stress well either.

"We're being careful, honey," Bill responded in an even tone.

Melinda had difficulty seeing Bill and Lani as a longtime couple. The two just didn't seem to fit. Bill, with his wire-rimmed glasses and slightly disheveled hair, had a serious, studious air. Lani, well, Lani was a cockatoo on steroids.

Jack closed the trunk and motioned everyone into the car. "Time to get cozy."

It was a tight fit, though more for the two in the back. Melinda moved her seat all the way forward to give Bill as much legroom as possible.

"You know the way?" Melinda asked Jack.

Jack shot her a wink. "GPS and I are on a first-name basis."

"I can tell you the best route to our house in Walker." From her position only a foot or two away in the back seat, Lani leaned forward. "Once you get off 91, it gets a little tricky."

Not tricky for GPS, Melinda thought, but said nothing.

"I appreciate the offer." Jack smiled at Lani. "I've been to Walker, so I know the way, at least to the town."

"Who were you visiting?" Lani pressed. "I probably know him. Or her."

"Lani," was all Bill said.

"What?" Lani's voice rose as she turned back to her husband. "You know as well as I do that no one just happens to come to

Walker. You only come if you know someone there." She turned back to Jack. "Who is it?"

The muscle that had jumped in Jack's jaw earlier when he'd spoken with his mother jumped again.

Sensitive area, Melinda surmised. Worse, yappy dog Lani couldn't easily be shut down.

"Lani…" Melinda turned in her seat and took charge of the conversation as Jack pulled out of the rental car lot. "Let's let Jack concentrate on getting us out of here. While he does that, I'm curious how you and Bill originally met and got together. Did you have one of those meet-cutes? You know, like in the movies?"

Before Lani could answer, Melinda's phone began to play "Dancing Queen." Melinda smiled. That was Kate's ringtone.

Melinda knew she should have anticipated the call. As soon as she'd settled in her seat, she'd turned on Share ETA.

"Tell me you're not in the car with him." Worry filled Kate's normally calm voice.

"If I told you that, it would be a lie." Melinda understood her friend's apprehension. Heck, she herself had gone back and forth on whether this was a smart move.

Right now, being in the car with a stranger felt okay because Lani and Bill were there, too. But once the couple were dropped off in Walker, she would be alone with Jack.

As Lani squabbled with her husband over the heat flow in the back seat—apparently his seat got more of the air, but no, she didn't want Jack to pull over so they could switch seats—Melinda realized she was actually looking forward to the couple being out of the car.

"Mel, please, you're putting your life in danger."

"Did you complete your research?" Melinda knew enough time had passed that her friend would have already looked up Jack. Something she herself hadn't had time to do.

"Lucy and I both did. We've been texting each other since you notified us of your crazy plan."

"That's good." Conscious that she wasn't alone in the vehicle, Melinda kept her response vague. "Tell me."

"A family with that name owns a sawmill in Timberhaven. Appears respectable. The dad's name is Curtis. Curtis McPherson."

"Hold on a sec." Melinda turned to Jack. "What's your father's name?"

"Curtis." He flashed a smile. "Checking up on me, Melinda?"

"Checking up on him?" Lani interjected, her voice filled with curiosity. "Why would you do that?"

Melinda ignored the question. "What else?"

She sensed Jack listening even as he expertly navigated his way through heavy traffic.

"He's in the family picture on the sawmill's website, but it doesn't appear he's actively involved with the operation," Kate continued. "Lucy found a Jack McPherson on LinkedIn who is a managing partner at a New York City equity firm. Nothing criminal anywhere, at least not that either of us could find."

Melinda relaxed against the heated seat. "That's good news."

"Since you appear to have made up your mind, all I'll say is stay safe. I'm really sorry your plans fell through, Mel. I know how much you were looking forward to this trip."

Regret for what was obviously not meant to be wrapped around Melinda's heart and squeezed. Still, she managed an upbeat tone. "There'll be other trips. See you soon."

"It may not seem like it now, but something tells me this will be a Christmas you'll never forget."

Melinda slanted a glance at Jack's handsome profile.

"You're not wrong about that." She shook her head and chuckled. "Having my trip canceled at the last minute and then getting into a car with three strangers... Well, let's just say this holiday is already memorable."

CHAPTER THREE

The roads they traveled were familiar to Jack. He'd lived in the city for a handful of years and had flown out of JFK more times than he cared to count. After his first year in NYC, he'd gotten rid of his car and rented one, or hired a car and driver, whenever necessary.

"You seem to know your way around."

"Watch out for that cab!" Lani shrieked in Jack's ear as she grabbed the headrest on his seat.

"Where?" Melinda wondered what cab the woman referred to, as none was even close to their car.

"I see it." Jack spoke in a confident tone intended to reassure. The last thing he needed, or wanted, was a neurotic backseat driver for the next two hundred miles. "Don't worry, Lani. I live in the city. I know how to drive here. I'll get you home safely."

"Honey," Bill said in a calm voice, "you need to chill out. That cab was nowhere close to us."

Melinda glanced back as if unsure what drama might follow.

But it appeared Jack had inadvertently given Lani a new mystery to solve, and she latched on to it like a dog gone to point.

"You live here?" Lani asked. "In Queens?"

Jack smiled. "Close. In Manhattan. Upper West Side."

"If you live here, then why are you driving us home?"

Because I'm celebrating not having to go to Mexico.

Because Melinda is an attractive woman.

Because I have nothing better to do.

The last thought he dismissed as soon as it surfaced. He had friends, and there were loads of activities in the city at this time of year.

Even though he wasn't at all disappointed that he wouldn't be spending the holidays in Mexico, he was in the mood for something different.

Even if that was only a family cabin in the woods.

"It doesn't make sense," Lani added when he didn't immediately respond.

He knew the woman wouldn't give up until he answered her question, so he made eye contact in the rearview mirror at the next red light. "My family has a cabin in the White Mountains. I'm headed there."

"From Mexico to the mountains." Bill spoke before Lani could comment, a smile in his voice. "If I got to pick, I'd go with the mountains."

"You never wanted to go to Mexico," Lani shot back. "You're not even disappointed our plans blew up."

"I was okay with going." Bill sounded perplexed. "You didn't get any pushback from me."

"Well, isn't that romantic?" Sarcasm mixed with the hurt in Lani's voice. "No pushback."

"I imagine New York is amazing at this time of year." Unlike Lani's, Melinda's tone remained cheery.

"It is," Jack admitted.

"I have friends here who I often visit, but I've never come during the holidays."

The fact that she hadn't mentioned this before had Jack

slanting a glance in her direction. "I'm surprised you didn't call them."

"They would have picked me up and let me stay the night," Melinda admitted. "But Faith and Graham have a baby due any day, which is why they didn't go to Holly Pointe to celebrate Christmas this year as usual."

She must have sensed his continued confusion, because she added, "They also have twin girls and don't need an unexpected houseguest during this busy time."

Jack nodded. "Makes sense."

"Look." She pointed outside. "It's beginning to snow."

"What a surprise." His lips quirked in a wry smile.

"The snow and cold are exactly what I was hoping to leave behind this Christmas." She slanted a glance at the windshield just as the wipers kicked into service. "Instead, I'm heading back into the thick of things."

"We could turn around," he said, only half joking. "Head south. It wouldn't be Mexico, but there are beaches in Florida."

Melinda twisted in her seat to face Bill and Lani. "What do you say, guys? Up for a spontaneous road trip?"

"Oooh, that sounds exciting." Lani's eyes brightened. "What do you say, Bill?"

"Lani, sweetheart," Bill placed a hand over hers, "she's joking."

The woman's gaze shot to Melinda, who smiled and said, "He's right. Though it is tempting."

Lani expelled a heavy sigh. "I wish we were headed to the Keys."

"There'll be other trips," Bill consoled. "I promise."

"I suppose." Another sigh from Lani.

Melinda leaned her head back against the headrest as the wiper blades picked up speed to match the pace of the falling snow.

"What are your plans when you get back to Holly Pointe?" Jack asked.

"I'll probably go back to work at the diner." Melinda kept her gaze focused straight ahead as they continued on I-95. "Christmas is a busy time for all the businesses in Holly Pointe."

"You work at a diner?"

"Waitressing mostly, but there isn't any part of the business I can't handle."

Jack wasn't sure why he was so surprised. Maybe because he'd have guessed she worked in something like marketing, based on her quick wit. Though the way she dealt with difficult people and the outrage she'd shown when the gate agent was being mistreated made sense for a restaurant worker, too.

"I can't believe the diner let you take vacation during December. That has to be the busiest month of the entire year."

"True, but I gave my mom plenty of notice."

"Your mother? Is she the manager?"

"The owner."

Before Melinda could say more, Lani leaned forward, seizing center stage. "I just realized that you asked me how Bill and I met, and I never answered your question."

Jack concluded his other questions for Melinda would have to wait.

Lani was off to the races, speaking quickly as if unsure how much time she had to get out all the information.

"Bill and I met our junior year in college. We were lab partners." Lani paused for a moment.

In the rearview, Jack saw her glance at her husband before she continued.

"He was smart and so patient with me. Science of any kind is definitely not a strength of mine."

"Lani was so pretty and outgoing." Bill's lips tipped as if he was recalling that long-ago science class. "I didn't think I stood a chance."

"Obviously, you did. Who asked who out first?" Melinda asked, sounding genuinely interested.

Lani chuckled. "Twenty-seven years ago, girls waited for the guy to ask."

"Tell them the truth, Lani." The amusement in Bill's voice caught Jack's attention. "You asked me."

"Not on a date," Lani clarified. "I asked if you wanted to grab a coffee or something to drink after class. There was this cute coffee shop near campus, and it was freezing outside. I wanted a hot chocolate. I thought Bill might enjoy one, too."

"I hadn't dated much," Bill admitted, "and I never thought that anyone as pretty and popular as Lani would be interested in me. But having her ask me to go to the coffee shop with her gave me the courage to ask her out on a proper date. The rest, as they say, is history."

"We got married the December after we graduated from college." Lani's voice turned dreamy, and she laid her head against Bill's shoulder.

"You were young."

Melinda's comment mirrored what Jack was thinking.

"We were twenty-two." Bill chuckled. "Our middle son is now twenty-two. It didn't seem young at the time, but I know that if he came to us and said he wanted to marry his girlfriend, our knee-jerk reaction would be to say he's not old enough."

"How old are you, Melinda?" Lani asked bluntly.

"I'm thirty." Melinda spoke in a matter-of-fact tone.

"What about you, Jack?"

Jack hid a grin. For a second, he'd thought he was off the hotseat. He should have known better. "Thirty-two."

"Have either of you been married before?" Lani asked.

Before either he or Melinda could respond, Lani tapped him on the shoulder. "The exit to Clatonia is just ahead."

Jack waited, assuming there was a point to the observation.

"I'm sure you're eager to get where we're going. Normally, I'd be okay with pushing through without stopping, but I skipped breakfast and lunch. There's a lovely little café on Main Street. If we could just stop and grab something quick to eat, the rest of the drive would be so much more pleasant."

In the momentary silence that followed as Jack considered the request, Melinda's empty stomach emitted a loud growl.

Jack grinned. "I'd say we have a second."

He could have driven farther. The protein bar he'd eaten at the airport had sustained him until food was mentioned. Only now did he realize the two women weren't the only hungry ones in the car.

"Works for me." The exit off the highway came up quickly, and he took it.

"Lani and I have a distant cousin who lives in Clatonia," Bill informed them. "We were here several years back for a family reunion. Unless Generous Bites, the place my wife mentioned, has gone belly up in the last couple of years or changed owner-ship, it has good food."

"Sounds like a good place to check out." When it struck Jack that Melinda hadn't given the go-ahead—unless you counted the stomach growl—he glanced in her direction. "Okay with you if we give it a try?"

"Sure." She smiled and pulled out her phone, then shifted in her seat. "What did you say the name of the place is?"

"Generous Bites," Lani and Bill said at the same time, then laughed.

"Thanks."

Turning back to face front, Melinda started texting, undoubt-edly letting her friends know of the side trip. He wasn't offended by her caution. Rather, he found himself admiring her careful nature.

Though Melinda appeared to be relaxing, he had the sense that she was still not fully comfortable being with him. He under-stood. He had two younger sisters, and he certainly wouldn't want them hopping into a car with strangers they'd met at an airport.

Hopefully, as she got to know him, Melinda would understand that she didn't have anything to fear from him.

"After we order," Lani announced, "we can spend time getting to know each other better."

Jack hid a smile. While Melinda didn't have anything to fear from him, he couldn't say she was as safe from Lani.

Lani stepped out of the vehicle the second Jack pulled to the curb, tossing orders over her shoulder. "You guys grab a table. I need to hit the restroom."

The woman was through the door of Generous Bites before Melinda and the two men had had a chance to shut their car doors.

Melinda paused on the sidewalk to study the exterior of the café. She approved of the pristine white clapboard siding accentuated by a bright red door. The colored Christmas lights around the window and the wreath on the door sporting a perky green-and-white-striped ribbon added a nice festive touch.

The moment she stepped inside, with Jack holding the door, Melinda's already heightened senses were enticed by the aroma that included both the sweet and savory.

The hardwood floor gleamed, and the tables appeared to be made up of leftover pieces of salvaged wood.

"This place is darling," she murmured.

"Told ya." Lani, who'd made quick work of her visit to the ladies' room, slipped her hand around Bill's arm. "We always said we'd come back. I didn't think it'd be on our anniversary, but—"

"Today is your anniversary?" The hostess, a thin woman with a long face, bestowed a bright smile on Lani and Bill.

"It is. We were supposed to be celebrating in Mexico, but—"

And Lani was off, telling the woman practically every detail of the past four hours, ending with Jack being gracious and giving her and Bill a lift to Walker.

"I supposed we could have pushed right through," Lani admitted, "but I was starving, and Melinda's stomach was growling so loudly we couldn't even talk."

Melinda offered a faint smile when the waitress, whose name, she'd learned through Lani's conversation, was Nev, fixed her gaze on her.

Nev patted Melinda's shoulder. "Don't you worry. I guarantee when you leave here that tummy of yours will be happy."

When Nev gestured to a table, then strode off to get them menus, Melinda leaned close to Jack. "Be honest. Was my stomach growling that loudly?"

He shook his head. "Lani is exaggerating. I only heard it that one time."

Somewhat mollified, Melinda smiled, then took the chair Jack pulled out for her. The others sat just as Nev returned with menus.

"I'll be back in a few minutes to get your orders." Nev glanced around the booth. "Can I get you something to drink while you look?"

After taking their drink orders, Nev hurried off.

The café was busy but not packed. Then again, it was nearly two, hardly a peak mealtime.

"I know what I'm going to have." Lani set down her menu just as Melinda's phone, which she'd set on the table beside her, pinged.

Melinda responded to the text quickly, then turned back to her menu. Unlike Lani, she hadn't yet decided what to order.

A second later, her phone dinged again.

Inclining his head, Jack smiled. "Friends checking up on you?"

Last time, it had been Kate. This time, it was Lucy.

Melinda had texted both her location and that they'd stopped for a meal, but her friends had wanted to make sure all was well.

Her heart swelled with love for these two women who cared so much. Both were extremely busy this time of year. Kate oversaw a group of cabins that were popular among visitors—and always booked out a year in advance—while Lucy owned the Barns at Grace Hollow, a gorgeous events venue at the edge of Holly Pointe.

Everything still okay??? Lucy had texted.

Melinda smiled, wondering just when it was that Lucy had started using multiple question marks in her texts.

Responding immediately, because she knew her friend would worry if she didn't, Melinda texted back, *Just getting ready to order. I'll text you when we're back on the road.*

Once she got the thumbs-up emoji, Melinda set her phone on the table.

"They must think you're a really bad judge of character."

Melinda looked up, startled by Lani's comment. "Who?"

"Your friends." Lani gestured to the phone with a hand tipped with bright pink nails. "It's like they think you're some twelve-year-old kid with no common sense. Bill and I don't pose a threat to you. Or maybe they have nothing better to do than meddle."

"Lani, honey—" Bill began.

"My friends trust my judgment." Melinda heard the coolness in her tone, but was unable to warm it. "They simply want to make sure I'm okay."

Melinda slanted a glance at Jack, whose attention was riveted on the menu, before shifting it back to fix her gaze on Lani.

Her take on Lani—though she was still in the preliminary assessment phase—was that Lani was an outspoken, opinionated woman who often spoke before she thought.

Still, she didn't like the implication of what Lani had said—not regarding herself or her friends. She leaned forward and met Lani's gaze head on.

"Jack is a stranger to me, as are you and Bill. I am their friend, and they want to make sure I'm safe. It has nothing to do with my judgment. Or with them having nothing better to do. In fact, quite the opposite. Both are career women who are taking time from their busy schedules to check on me out of concern. You and I both know that some men who seem nice really aren't."

The vehemence in her tone didn't surprise her. Melinda didn't let anyone diss her friends.

Lani blinked.

The slight smile lifting Jack's lips told her he was listening. She wondered if he'd find it as amusing if he were the one Lani was zeroing in on.

"We all just met today," Melinda continued. "If you were alone, Lani, wouldn't Bill be concerned about you getting into a vehicle and traveling hundreds of miles with people you'd just met? Wouldn't he want to keep track of you on that trip?"

Lani blinked, her gaze shifting from Melinda to Jack, who had finally set down his menu. "I thought the two of you knew each other. I thought you were dating." She looked at her husband. "Isn't that what you thought, Bill?"

Bill just shrugged.

"Well, we're not dating. We're strangers."

"Good to know." Then Lani smiled brightly. "Looks like Nev is here to take our order. Is everyone ready?"

CHAPTER FOUR

After taking their orders quickly and with great efficiency, Nev left with promises to bring tea and soda refills.

Melinda embraced the ordering as a brief respite from Lani's promised interrogation. The trouble was, she couldn't figure out how to put the woman off without coming across as rude.

She didn't mind talking about herself, sharing amusing anecdotes about her childhood and work life. The thing with Lani, or at least what she'd observed so far, was she liked to dig deep. That, in Melinda's mind, was too much too soon, considering they'd just met.

Even the age thing. She didn't mind telling anyone how old she was, though hitting thirty had been jarring. What would the next question be? How much did she earn in a year? Or maybe when the last time was she'd had sex? Just the thought of that question made her smile, imagining the shock on Lani's face if she answered honestly and said—

"I assume you're single," Lani said.

Melinda didn't let her elaborate. "Why would you assume that?"

"Well…" Lani blinked, obviously surprised by the question.

"You were traveling to Mexico alone. If you're married, I assume your husband would be with you." By the time she finished speaking, Lani's confidence had returned.

"I could just as easily have been headed to meet friends for a girls' trip."

Lani gave a reluctant nod. "I suppose. Were you headed to meet friends?"

Give the woman an inch, and she asked another question, Melinda thought. "No. This was just a getaway from the cold for me."

"You said you're not married now. Were you ever married?"

Jack pulled out his phone and appeared to be emailing or texting. Since he was busy, Melinda was on her own in dealing with Lani. She couldn't look to him for assistance. Jack was apparently smart enough to know that if Lani got diverted, she would likely drill down on *his* life.

"No." Melinda kept her tone matter-of-fact. "I've never been married."

To Melinda's surprise, Lani shifted her focus to Jack.

"Jack," Lani said. When he continued to focus on his phone and didn't respond, she said more loudly, "Jack."

He looked up. "Is the food here?"

Melinda admired his aplomb. He wasn't about to make this easy for Lani.

"Not yet," Lani said. "Though it shouldn't be long."

"That's great," he said. "Because I'm starting to get hungry. Stopping was a good idea, as was eating at this café. How long ago did you say it was that you last ate here?"

"Three years, I think." Bill answered the question Jack had posed to Lani, but he glanced at his wife, seeking confirmation.

"Three years ago, this coming summer." Lani smiled her thanks when Nev refilled her glass of iced tea.

"Did Nev wait on you back then?" Jack asked.

Melinda knew he couldn't possibly be interested in who had

been Lani and Bill's server three years ago, but he was playing it smart. Every question he asked Lani took the place of one she'd be asking him.

"It wasn't you," Lani said to Nev, who'd paused by the table. "It was a tall woman with hair almost as carroty red as Melinda's."

Carroty red? Melinda blinked, then frowned. She'd never been a carrottop. Not even when she was a young girl. But she wasn't about to draw Lani's attention back to her by commenting.

"That would be Erin. She's the manager now." Nev smiled. "She isn't working today, but I'll tell her you came back and remembered her. She'll like hearing that. We get a lot of repeat business because of word of mouth."

"Nev," a loud voice called out. "Order is up."

Nev flashed a smile. "Sounds like your food is ready. Back in a sec."

It really was only a second, or maybe it just seemed that way because Jack kept up a running commentary about what he'd ordered and what he'd almost ordered until the food was on the table.

Melinda had gone with one of the specialty burgers with fries for her side. She picked up a highly seasoned fry from her plate and bit into it, resisting the urge to close her eyes as the seasonings came together in an explosion of tantalizing flavors. "These are fabulous."

Jack smiled. "Tell me how you really feel."

She grinned and picked up another fry. Except this time, instead of eating it, she studied it. "I wish my mother would consider serving something like these."

"Your mother?" Lani asked.

"She owns a diner in Holly Pointe," Melinda explained.

"A diner that doesn't serve burgers and fries?" A look of mock horror crossed Jack's face. "Say it isn't so."

Melinda chuckled, then dipped the fry into a small silver cup of ranch dressing. "We have burgers and crinkle fries, but not fries like these." She glanced down at her avocado burger served on a brioche bun. Not only was the grilled patty topped with avocado crema, there was avocado in the burger as well. "I think our patrons would love something like this, too, but my mother isn't big on changing up the menu."

Melinda kept expecting Lani to jump into the conversation, but about then, their son texted to make sure they'd arrived safely in Mexico. Lani and Bill were now involved in a three-way text with him while attempting to eat.

"How many years has your mother owned the café?" Jack asked.

"Over twenty-five." Melinda popped another fry into her mouth.

"I guess if it ain't broke, why fix it?"

Melinda smiled at the phrase that was her mother's favorite comeback whenever she offered a suggestion. The truth was, what had worked for so many years wasn't working any longer. At least not as well as it once had.

While Rosie's Diner remained a favorite among the seniors in Holly Pointe—where else could you get a cup of coffee for a buck?—visitors and even many locals weren't beating down the door in droves as they once had.

"I suppose." Melinda kept her tone offhand.

The details of her mother's recent business struggles—and her resistance to change—were no one's business but family's.

"You don't sound convinced."

Melinda gave a slight shrug, then took a sip of her Coke, liking the nice jolt the caffeine and sugar gave her system. "Thank you for stopping so we could eat. I'm beginning to feel almost human again."

"I didn't realize how hungry I was until we walked through the door." He glanced around. "This place has a comfortable ambience. Nothing fancy, but a cool vibe."

"A cool vibe is exactly what Rosie's Diner needs."

"Have you thought what changes you'd make if you were in charge?"

"Rosie's is my mother's baby, and she's nowhere near ready to turn it over to me."

"Would you take it, if she did?"

The question reminded her of something Lani would say and made Melinda smile. "I'm not sure."

"Why the hesitation?" He took another bite of his burger and chewed.

"The restaurant business is tough. Long hours. High cost of supplies. Continual staffing issues."

"What kind of staffing issues?"

"Holly Pointe isn't a one-restaurant town. There are lots of other businesses, all looking for reliable help." Melinda nearly added that servers went where the tips were, and as business at Rosie's had taken a downturn, they'd flocked to places like Jingle Shells and Holly Jolly's, where business was brisk, and tips were good. "We have a lot of senior business. They come in to eat and often stay to play cards. Many are still living in the 1960s or '70s in terms of tipping. They seem to think a dollar is a fair tip."

"That's tough." Jack's gaze turned thoughtful. "I mean, it's good for a restaurant to have a loyal clientele, and it's great for a community to have a gathering place for seniors, but you and your servers still need to make ends meet."

"Exactly." Melinda let her gaze sweep the dining area. "I've spoken with our city manager about turning the empty VFW hall into a senior center. It could be a place where those in the community could go during the year to meet up and play cards. Maybe put in a pool table or shuffleboard table. It would be good for the building and good for the community."

"And it would get them out of the diner."

She laughed. "Exactly."

"I'm glad you accepted my offer."

Melinda inclined her head.

"Having you along has made the drive much more pleasurable." Putting his burger down, he sobered. "I hope you're not worried about me anymore. I'd really hate for you to be concerned during this long drive that you've made a mistake getting in a car with me."

"I'm just a cautious person by nature."

"What can I do to make you feel more comfortable?"

"Can I see your driver's license?"

Sitting back, he gave her a quizzical smile. "My driver's license?"

It was clear by his response that while he'd made the offer, he hadn't expected her to come back with a specific request.

"That way I know for certain that the name you gave me and the story about where you live are true."

Before she finished speaking, he pulled out his wallet and slipped out his driver's license, handing it to her.

"This photo is surprisingly good." Of course, it was hard to take a bad picture when you had good bones, a mass of dark hair and arresting blue eyes.

His lips quirked upward. "Thanks, I guess. I've never thought much about the photo."

"You would if they got the lighting wrong and you looked like a ghost." Before placing the license into his outstretched hand, Melinda took note of his name, age and New York address.

He slipped the license back into his wallet, then held out his hand.

"What?" she asked, puzzled.

"I want to see yours now."

"Why?"

"I could say because I want to make sure you are who you say you were, but the truth is…"

"The truth is?" she prompted.

A grin spread across his face. "I want to see what you look like as a ghost."

The dishes were cleared from the table, and they were done except for the check, when singing across the room had them turning in their seats. Nev strode toward them, carrying a piece of chocolate cake as big as a dinner plate topped with white frosting and crushed candy canes. A candle flickered in the middle.

Two other servers—a man and a woman—flanked her, offering broad smiles as they sang, "Happy anniversary to you," slightly off-key.

"It's this lovely couple's twenty-fifth wedding anniversary today." Nev spoke in a loud voice that filled the dining area. "Let's give them a big round of applause."

Applause, along with a few whistles, had tears filling Lani's eyes as Nev set the dessert before her, and her two associates added plates, forks, napkins and a cake knife.

"Thank you." Lani brought a hand to her throat and blinked rapidly. "This is unexpected and…wonderful."

"I cut you a piece big enough for all of you to share." Nev glanced around the table. "How about some coffee to go with the cake? The cake and coffee are on the house."

"We'd love some, and thank you for all of this." Bill swept an arm that included not only the dessert, but Nev and her associates.

"Enjoy." Nev smiled, then left to get the coffee.

"I know you said you were going to celebrate when you got back to Walker." Melinda accepted the generous piece of cake that Lani dished up and handed to her. "How are you going to top this?"

Bill glanced at his wife with a twinkle in his eye, then brushed a kiss across her cheek. "I've got some ideas."

Lani's giggle reminded Melinda of her teenage niece.

"No need to explain further." Melinda picked up a fork and found herself fighting a pang of envy.

Her father had died when she was a baby. Her mother's second marriage hadn't lasted.

"What's your secret?" The question was out of Melinda's mouth before she realized what she was asking.

Nev returned with the coffee, then left them to their conversation and dessert.

Lani shifted her gaze and lowered her fork. She glanced at her husband. "Lots of love and a willingness to admit when you're wrong."

"Never letting the sun set on your anger," Bill added.

"You remember." Pleasure spread across Lani's face.

"Remember what?" Melinda asked.

"A maid at the motel where we spent our wedding night told us that the secret to a long and happy marriage is to never let the sun set on your anger." Lani turned to her husband. "I think we've done a pretty good job in that regard."

"I can only think of one or two times where that didn't happen." Bill reached over and covered her free hand with his, giving it a squeeze. "Here's to another twenty-five."

Melinda looked away when Lani wrapped her arms around Bill's neck for a kiss.

Instead, she focused on Jack, who was eating his dessert.

"Have your parents been married a long time?" she asked, wondering why she felt like Lani even though she was asking only a simple question.

Jack thought for a moment. "Thirty-five years."

"Are they happy?" Melinda wasn't sure why she asked or why it mattered.

"Yes." Jack added a nod. "Not only are they still in love, they're good friends, and they respect each other."

Melinda recalled his tense expression when he'd been speaking with his mother. "Is your family close?"

"Yes." Jack took a bite of cake, an indication that he had no more to say on the matter.

"I want to believe in happily ever after, but—"

Before she could say more, Lani broke in. "It's starting to snow again. We probably should get back on the road. I wouldn't want you two to get stuck after you drop us off."

Jack grinned. "Why do I get the feeling that this eagerness is more about your desire to embrace the anniversary celebration Bill has planned at home than snow-packed roads?"

CHAPTER FIVE

After delivering Lani and Bill to their home in Walker, Jack pointed the car toward Holly Pointe. They were three hours from Melinda's hometown when snow began falling in earnest. Thankfully, the number of vehicles on the road were now confined to a few semis and their midget of a car.

Jack gripped the steering wheel, and his gaze remained firmly fixed on the white curtain in front of them. The conversation he and Melinda had enjoyed after dropping off Lani and Bill had dwindled as keeping the vehicle on the road demanded Jack's entire concentration.

A ping had Melinda looking down at the phone in her lap.

Jack didn't even glance over.

Melinda quickly read Kate's latest text.

State police say don't travel. Whiteout conditions. Major accident outside of Frost. Road closed to northbound traffic.

They should be hitting Frost in a matter of minutes. Melinda turned to Jack. "We should take the next exit."

Before he could respond, she told him what Kate had texted.

"Just in time." He took an exit that Melinda hadn't even

known was there until they were right on top of it. "This is the last exit before Frost."

Melinda expelled a breath. "I couldn't read the sign. Do you know what town this is?"

Keeping his gaze on the road, he said, "If it's the last one before Frost, and I'm pretty sure it is, then it will be Wilbur."

"We shouldn't have stopped to eat." Though it was pointless now, Melinda wondered if they would have gotten ahead of the storm if they'd continued on.

Jack lifted a shoulder. "We were hungry."

"Have you ever been to this town before?"

"I don't believe so."

"I wonder if we'll be able to find a couple of rooms," Melinda mused. "I sure don't want to sleep in the car."

"That makes two of us." Jack slanted a quick glance in her direction. "If you can get reception, why don't you see what lodging there is and which ones have a couple of rooms available?"

"Are you sure we're headed toward Wilbur?"

Jack gestured with his head. "There was a sign a mile back. Barely visible, but yes, that's where we're headed."

The only place Melinda found that had a vacancy was a B&B in town. She asked if the woman could hold a couple of rooms for them, but lost the connection before she could receive confirmation.

Hoping for the best, Melinda plugged the address into her phone. "Turn right at the next light."

Jack slanted a sideways glance. "They have two rooms?"

"I think so, but we got cut off, and now her phone is ringing busy." Melinda resisted the urge to sigh. "If not, we'll just have to go with plan B."

"Which is?"

"Have you ever slept in a car?"

He laughed and turned right at the light.

~

"I'm sorry." Regret blanketed the older woman's face. "We only have one room available."

"I don't mind sharing—" Jack began, even as Melinda gave her head a little shake.

Though Jack believed his driver's license and her time in the car with him had convinced Melinda he wasn't a serial killer, it was clear that she wasn't about to share a room with a man she'd just met.

"You take the room," he told Melinda, then turned to the woman with the tight brown curls who'd introduced herself as Claudia Kastens. The man at her side was her husband, Kent.

Though Kent, a balding man who appeared to be in his early fifties had been with her when she'd opened the door, it was clear by how he hung back now that this B&B stuff was his wife's purview.

It had also been clear to Jack the instant he'd seen the old two-story home why a room was still available. Though the porch was clear of clutter, the exterior needed painting, and there was nothing to indicate this was anything more than a single-family home.

"All but one room is taken, then?" Jack asked in a pleasant, conversational tone. If he was going to be relegated to the car, he was going to spend as much time in the warmth as possible.

"We only have the one," Claudia admitted, then quickly added, "For right now, anyway. Once our son Grant leaves for college next fall, we'll open up his room to guests."

"We got into the B&B business only recently." Claudia cast a look back at her husband. "Kent works for a small manufacturing plant here in Wilbur. Business has been slow, and since orders are down, most of those who worked the floor were laid off for December. Renting out a room helps keep the lights on."

"Being laid off, especially at this time of year, has to be difficult." The sympathy in Melinda's voice was reflected on her face.

Kent shrugged. "Yes, but I tell myself that at least I still have a job. Still, going without a paycheck for a month, especially at this time of year, bites."

"I bet." Melinda glanced around. "You've got a lovely home. I'm glad you have the one room available."

Melinda shifted her focus to Jack then, the look in her hazel eyes brooking no argument. "We'll take shifts in the car. I'll set an alarm for four hours, then come out and get you, and we'll switch."

No way was he letting her sleep in the car. Before they'd left Generous Bites, she'd changed into the clothes she'd packed for her return to snowy Vermont once she left the Mexican sun. But her coat was light, and her jeans and long-sleeved tee weren't made for a night in a car during a snowstorm.

Jack thought quickly, considering options, discarding one, then quickly moving to another. As the couple had come from a living room where the television still blared, they probably wouldn't go for him sleeping on their sofa. He thought of the window he'd noticed on the third level.

"What about your attic?" Jack kept his tone casual, feeling his way.

"We cleaned it out good last fall," Claudia admitted. "I think the only thing left is some old camping equipment. We thought about making it another bedroom for guests, but the city told us we needed a second way out in case of fire." Claudia glanced at Kent. "We weren't sure we'd be able to recoup the investment."

"I understand. There's a lot of material and labor involved in constructing a fire escape." Jack paused. "At the moment, I'm more worried about freezing to death than dying in a fire. I'd be grateful if you'd let me rent your attic for the night."

When Claudia hesitated, Jack pressed forward. "I did plenty of camping with my family growing up. Not to mention all the times my brother and I pitched a tent in our bedroom. Sleeping on the floor is not a problem." He flashed what he hoped was a persuasive smile. "It's worth two hundred to me."

"To sleep on a floor?" Claudia's voice rose, and at any other time, her expression would have been laughable. "We only charge seventy-five a night for a room with a bed."

"Because you've been told you can't rent out that spot and you'd be making an exception for me, the two hundred is worth it to me. I'd appreciate it since Melinda will insist on taking shifts in the car. I really don't want her out in the cold."

Claudia's expression softened as her gaze settled on Melinda briefly before shifting back to Jack. "You can stay in the attic, but I'm not taking any money from you. Kent will get Grant's sleeping bag for you, and you can pretend you're camping."

"Thank you. Seriously, thank you." Relief washed over Jack. Now he wouldn't have to argue with Melinda about splitting time in the car.

"If you could pay the seventy-five dollars for the room before we show you upstairs?" Two bright spots of pink dotted Claudia's cheeks as her gaze shifted to Melinda. "We got burned once and—"

"I totally understand." Melinda's voice rang warm with reassurance. She shook her head when Jack reached for his wallet. "I'll pay for the room I'll be sleeping in."

Jack held up his hands in a gesture of surrender. She'd allowed him to pay for lunch. He could already tell he had no chance of winning this argument.

Scooping up his leather duffel, Jack turned to Kent. "Ready when you are."

The bed boasted a down comforter and a mattress that Goldilocks would have decreed perfect. Melinda supposed she could have ventured up to the attic to check out Jack's digs, but instead, she sat on the bed and texted her friends in a group chat.

Lucy had married Trevor, an old friend from her childhood, last January. After Lucy had confirmed Melinda was safe, she explained she and Trevor were at a party.

When Lucy said good night, Melinda and Kate switched to a one-on-one chat.

You're not at the party? Melinda texted. She knew that Kate would have been invited.

I thought about it, but I've been swamped with the cabins.

There was truth to that, Melinda knew, but it wasn't all. *Mostly couples???*

The extra question marks she added made Melinda think of Lucy, and she couldn't help smiling.

Even Zach and Derek were bringing dates, came Kate's reply a second later.

Since Derek was her brother, Melinda knew the woman he was dating. It had been one of the reasons she'd decided to spend the holidays in Mexico. While she was happy that her mother and Derek currently had romantic partners, being with the group made her feel like the odd woman out in her own family. *If I was there, we could have gone to the party together.*

You should be in sunny Mexico lounging on the beach.

Yep, Melinda quickly agreed. *You should be with me.*

I wish I could have gone with you. but, you know, the cabins...

I know.

How's the stranger?

So far, so good. Melinda thought of Jack. Yes, the drive had been pleasurable.

I did more research. His family is rolling in $$$, and so is he.

Doesn't surprise me. Melinda thought about how he'd forked over five hundred dollars in cash to get the car and then how willing he'd been to pay top dollar to sleep on an attic floor.

They texted back and forth for another ten minutes before

ending the conversation. Both had had full days, and Melinda had hardly slept the night before. Not only because she'd had to get up early to catch the bus to the airport, but because she'd been excited to start her vacation.

Plugging in her phone to charge, Melinda slid under the covers. She must have fallen asleep instantly, because when she opened her eyes, sunlight streamed through the open window.

After taking a quick shower, she pulled on the clothes she'd worn last night—the only warm ones she'd packed—and headed for the stairs with her suitcase.

Laughter and voices filtered up the stairs. The tantalizing scent of coffee and something more had her quickening her step.

A boy who looked about seventeen brushed past her on his way out the front door. "Sorry," he said when his shoulder clipped hers. "Snow to push."

He was out the door before she could reply. *Must be Grant,* she thought and turned in the direction of the kitchen, where she found Claudia, Kent and Jack sitting around the table.

Jack pushed back his chair and stood. "Good morning. How did you sleep?"

When he rounded the table, Melinda thought for one horrifying instant that he was going to kiss her. When he only pulled out a chair for her, she wondered why that particular thought had crossed her mind.

"We're a little informal here this morning." Claudia was now on her feet. "I made my coconut almond French toast casserole. My entire family raves about it, but if you don't like coconut or have an issue with nuts, we have several different cereals, or I can—"

"The casserole sounds intriguing. I love both coconut and almonds, and I'm a huge fan of French toast." Melinda eyed the amount of casserole on the men's plates and wondered how there could be any left.

She liked the way the casserole looked on the plates, with a sprinkling of powdered sugar and berries on top. It was something that she could see going over well at Rosie's.

"You're in for a treat." Claudia smiled. "Coffee?"

"Please." Melinda smiled. "The bed was very comfortable."

Only then did she remember that one of them at the table hadn't slept in a bed last night. Melinda cast Jack an apologetic glance. "Sorry. How was the floor?"

"Surprisingly comfortable." His gaze slid to Claudia and Kent, and he lifted his cup. "Much, much better than a cold car."

"Speaking of cars," Kent said. "I told Grant to brush yours off while he's out there shoveling."

"Thanks. That's nice of him. Have the plows been through?" Jack asked just as Claudia set a large slice of casserole before Melinda.

Not wanting to interrupt, Melinda smiled her thanks to Claudia, a smile that widened as soon as she took her first bite.

The buttery coconut almond crust was the perfect contrast to the fluffy texture of the bread. Melinda could see why this dish was a family favorite.

"The plow came through around six thirty. We're on a major roadway, so we always get done first." Kent took a bite of casserole and chewed thoughtfully. "You know how it is in these parts —doesn't take long after a storm for things to get back to normal."

After growing up in Vermont, there was plenty Melinda could say about the weather and roads, but everyone around this table was as familiar with how things worked in the winter as she was, so she focused on savoring the amazing food and enjoying the strong, dark roast.

"You mentioned this morning that you're from northern New Hampshire." Kent looked at Jack with interest. "Where exactly?"

"Timberhaven."

Kent glanced at his wife. "Small world."

"You know the town?" Jack asked, fork poised in the air.

"Our eldest son, Scott, lives there." Claudia smiled. "His wife, Sarah, is from the area." Claudia shifted her gaze to Jack. "Her name was Sarah Milleson. Sarah Kastens now."

Jack appeared to consider the name, then shook his head. "I'm afraid not."

"Sarah is a lovely girl." Claudia took a sip of coffee. "She teaches middle school."

"What about Scott?" Melinda asked. "Is he also a teacher?"

"No. Right now, he's working for Atomic Car Parts. He's been trying to get on at Timberhaven Sawmill," Claudia confided. "They're the largest—and according to Scott—the best employer in town, but openings are few and far between."

"Scott is a hard worker and very self-motivated," Kent chimed in. "He'd love to get into anything to do with parts, but he can't even get an interview with Glenn Oaks."

"Glenn Oaks?" Melinda asked.

"Sorry. Scott has mentioned him so often, it's easy to think everyone knows who he is. Glenn is the head of human resources at Timberhaven." Kent's gaze met hers, and Melinda saw the pride in his eyes. "My son would be an asset to any organization. He just needs a chance to prove it."

Melinda glanced at Jack. If her intel was correct, the sawmill was his family business. She wondered if he would mention the connection.

"Any idea why he can't get an interview?" Jack kept his tone casual, displaying only mild interest.

"Scott doesn't know. I mean, he's never been in any trouble. He's always gotten great performance evaluations wherever he's worked." Kent shrugged. "The only thing we can figure is not enough experience and no in."

Jack arched a brow. "In?"

"No one on the inside who can vouch for him. You know, for his character, his work ethic, stuff like that." Kent shook his head.

"We're not people who have connections like that. Sarah's folks are teachers, so—"

"No in," Melinda filled in the rest of the sentence.

"Exactly." Kent expelled a breath. "But our boy is persistent. I've told him, 'You just keep trying. Maybe they'll get sick of seeing your application and hire you.'"

"Or they may tell him to quit applying." Claudia expelled a heavy sigh.

"Or that," Kent agreed.

"Will you be seeing Scott and Sarah at Christmas?" Jack asked.

"We're not sure what we're doing just yet." Claudia took a long sip of coffee. "Grant is playing in a basketball tournament in Clatonia this weekend. That, along with Kent being out of work, has thrown a wrench into our holiday plans."

"If you have a day free, you might want to consider a day trip to Holly Pointe. There are so many activities for teens and adults. Something for everyone," Melinda added.

"Is that where the two of you will be celebrating Christmas?" Claudia rose, then returned to the table to refill everyone's coffee mugs.

"I'll definitely be there." Melinda explained about her Mexico vacation plans falling through and gave a brief synopsis of how she and Jack met.

"I didn't realize the two of you were strangers." Claudia chuckled and shook her head. "No wonder you didn't want to share a bed."

"Riding in a car with someone I've just met is enough of a risk for me," Melinda said in an equally light tone.

"She has nothing to worry about with me." Jack smiled at her, giving her his full attention for the first time this morning.

Melinda met his gaze and felt the punch. When she felt herself blushing, she pushed back her chair and rose.

"This was so good, but we should be getting on the road." Melinda turned to Claudia. "How much do I owe for breakfast?"

"Not a thing. It's part of the package."

Melinda began shaking her head before Claudia finished. Seventy-five dollars was not enough for the lovely room *and* breakfast, especially when Claudia would be cleaning up after two people. "Yes, but we only paid for a package for one room, and really we were two."

Taking a twenty-dollar bill out of her purse, Melinda pushed it into Claudia's hand. "I insist."

Claudia studied her for a long moment. "I'm guessing by that look in your eye it's not going to do me any good to argue."

"You're right. It won't do you any good." Melinda softened the words with a smile.

"But you," Claudia leveled a gaze on Jack, "I will not accept any money from you, not for sleeping on the floor. Understand?"

"Yes, ma'am." Jack nodded. "I see where you're coming from, and I won't argue with you."

Melinda had just gotten settled in the car when she surprised Jack by reaching for the door.

He placed his hand lightly on her arm. "Where are you going?"

"I left my charger in the room."

"I'll get it." Jack pushed open his door. "Your feet got wet just getting to the car. While I'm gone, crank up the heat and pretend the snow is white sand and the sun shining down is hot on your face."

"I've got a good imagination." She smiled back at him. "Not that good."

"I'll be right back."

"I left it plugged in next to the bed," she told him.

Jack gave two quick raps on the front door.

"I'm sorry to interrupt, but Melinda left her charger," he told Claudia when the woman opened the door.

"I'm glad she remembered it now and not when she got home." Claudia motioned him inside. "Do you know where she left it?"

He nodded.

"Since it appears you know where it is, you might as well go upstairs and get it."

Jack glanced down at his wet feet. "You sure?"

"Positive."

After carefully wiping his boots on the mat just inside the door, he climbed the stairs to the second floor.

Claudia's response—or, rather, lack of response, told Jack that she hadn't entered the bedroom yet, or she'd have seen what he'd slipped in there right before he'd walked out the door.

Jack found the charger exactly where Melinda had said he'd find it. He couldn't believe he hadn't noticed it when he'd left the note on the nightstand along with two one-hundred-dollar bills and his business card. The note was a simple thanks for their hospitality, along with instructions to have Scott call Glenn Oaks and say Jack had recommended him.

He knew they wouldn't take the cash from him. Knew they'd push it back at him. But he also knew that they really needed the money.

And Scott, well, the boy deserved a chance. If he really was as solid a worker as Kent believed, Timberhaven would be lucky to have him.

A win-win for everyone concerned.

While it was on his mind, Jack texted Glenn.

Hi, Glenn. Scott Kastens will be calling you. I'd appreciate you finding a place for him. Thx.

Then, with Melinda's charger in hand, Jack descended the stairs and headed outside to the car.

CHAPTER SIX

They'd barely driven twenty miles when Melinda's phone dinged.

Jack grinned. "Someone wants to make sure you're still alive."

Melinda's thumbs flew as she answered Kate's text, then she shifted her gaze back to Jack. "Holly Pointe got snow, but Kate says the roads have been cleared, so there shouldn't be any delays."

"You know, if there is any sort of a delay, you'll have some explaining to do."

Melinda rolled her eyes. "They're not like that. They just want me home safe."

"I'll get you there safely."

"What are you going to do then?" Melinda settled back against the heated seat, enjoying the warmth and surprisingly smooth ride over snow-packed roadways.

He slanted her a sideways glance. "What do you mean?"

"Your entire family is having fun while you're left back here."

"You sound as if spending the holidays here is a chore, when it's anything but." He smiled. "I enjoy winter, and it doesn't seem like Christmas to me without snow on the ground."

She nearly mentioned missing his brother's wedding, but

didn't want to rub salt in the wound, so she tried to focus on the positive. "Do you have close family that you can be with?"

"'Fraid not."

He sounded almost cheery, but how could that be?

"What about friends?"

"Are you worried about me, Melinda?" His teasing tone hit her wrong.

She lifted her chin. "I just know how lonely the holidays can be."

"You're right," he agreed, his expression turning serious. "I have a few friends left in Timberhaven, but they'll be spending this last week before Christmas with their families, or with their girlfriends."

"No old girlfriends hanging around in New Hampshire hoping for your return?"

His fingers tightened almost imperceptibly on the steering wheel. If she'd had something more interesting to watch than him, she might not have noticed.

"They're all married. Or about to be married."

Melinda inclined her head. "Did you ever get close?"

He hesitated for a long moment. Uncertain what to say? Or unsure how much to share? "I was in a serious relationship once."

"What happened?"

"She changed her mind."

"I'm sorry. Is there a chance you'll get back together?"

"Well, she's marrying my brother, so I'm going with, 'no.'" Jack offered up a humorless laugh. "Even if that wasn't happening, we wouldn't be getting back together, which is why my reluctance to attend their wedding makes no sense. It's illogical. I don't want Natalie back, but for some reason, the fact that she broke up with me and then started dating my brother—and that the whole family is good with it—still stings."

Melinda wasn't sure which of them was more surprised by his admission.

He waved a hand. "Sorry. Forget I said anything. I don't normally babble. Especially about personal stuff."

Having been down this road before, Melinda understood how much a breakup could hurt, even when you knew the split was for the best. And how good it could feel to share confusing feelings. "Did she break up with you for your brother?"

For a second, she thought he might not answer, then he shook his head. "No. They started dating about a year after our breakup. Six months later, they were engaged."

"Why did you break up?"

When silence filled the interior of the car for several long seconds, she wondered if she'd overstepped.

Jack blew out a breath. "When we started dating, we wanted the same things. A life in NYC, where we could develop our careers. For a couple years, we did that. But where some couples grow together, we grew apart. Natalie started talking more about kids and family."

"You didn't want that?"

"I didn't want that right then. I felt like we were young and had time. I was making a lot of connections and knew that within another year or so, I'd be able to start my own firm, which I did. I asked her to wait."

"And she didn't?"

"Actually, she did, for another year. But when I still wasn't ready, she decided she was done waiting. She knew what she wanted and that if I didn't want to give it to her, someone else would. She was right. I just didn't expect the someone else to be my brother."

Melinda knew that had to be a bitter pill. "Did you know your brother liked her?"

"No, and to be fair, I don't think either of them planned it. They'd always gotten along, my whole family loved her—still do, of course—and I've always been grateful for that."

"Still has to be difficult."

He shrugged. "Natalie and Sam have similar interests. They both studied architecture in school, they both love being outside in nature, they're both funny and good with people, and both are eager to start a family. It makes sense, in a way. Sam can give her what I couldn't."

"Maybe you could have," Melinda suggested, "given more time?"

"No, I don't think so. Looking back, I think I liked Natalie for the ways she was similar to me. But that wasn't the full picture of who she is. She is the woman who wants to live in the city and pursue a career, but she's also a lot of other things. I never really saw her full, true self. My brother does. He sees her the way she wants to be seen."

"Did she see you like you want to be seen?"

"I'm not sure. I'd like to think no, but sometimes I worry that maybe she did." He cast her a sideways glance. "How about you? You said you've never been married. Did you ever come close to taking a trip down the aisle?"

Melinda considered how much to say about her relationship with Alex, a man she'd dated when she'd lived in Burlington. She didn't particularly like revisiting that time, but Jack had been forthright with her. Could she be less with him?

"When I lived in Burlington, I dated someone who asked me to marry him. I said no. While we had many common interests and I enjoyed spending time with him, I didn't love him." Her heart twisted as she recalled the hurt on Alex's face and how he'd begged her to take more time to think about his proposal.

It had been clear to her that more time wouldn't change her feelings. She'd broken it off and, in doing so, had broken his heart.

Thinking of Jack's comments of his former fiancée had her wondering… If Alex had seen her for who she was, wouldn't he have recognized she wasn't ready to settle down? Instead, he'd tried to force the relationship.

"Do you stay in touch?"

The question pulled her from her reverie. "No. There was no point. He wanted my love, and that was something I was unable to give. Trying to force a friendship felt like I'd only be hurting him more."

Melinda shifted in her seat and thought not about Alex, but about Jack and his brother. "Have you forgiven your brother for marrying your former fiancée?"

A muscle in Jack's jaw jumped. "There is nothing to forgive. Like I said, Natalie and I split long before she and Sam started dating."

On the surface, his reluctance to attend the wedding was, as he'd stated, illogical. Then again… "Did Sam ask for your blessing before he started dating her?"

"No." Jack expelled a breath. "I wish he had, just so I could have told him it was fine."

"And if he had, you'd have known that he respected your feelings."

"We all make mistakes," Jack said simply. "Sam should have asked. Once I heard they were dating, I should have contacted him and cleared the air. Instead, we both pretended everything was okay when it clearly wasn't."

Melinda understood regret. "I should have told Alex long before he proposed that I didn't see a future for us."

Reaching over, Jack took her hand and gave it a squeeze. "Going forward, we'll both do better."

Changing the subject from ex-lovers and regrets, Jack started telling her stories about growing up in Timberhaven and his years of living and working in New York City.

"It sounds as if you really like your work."

"I do. It's interesting and fast-paced." Jack offered a rueful smile. "I realize it might sound boring to you, but I enjoy overseeing the sourcing of potential investment opportunities and assessing the potential returns associated with each investment. I

CHRISTMAS MOON OVER HOLLY POINTE | 59

especially like the fundraising part." He paused for a moment. "Actually, there isn't any part of the business I don't like."

"You're lucky to do work that you feel passionate about and that fulfills you." Financial, well, *stuff* had never been a strength of Melinda's, but she liked the way his eyes lit up when he spoke about his job. "Why did you name your company after your home town?"

"The other names I considered were already trademarked." Jack relaxed against the back of his seat. "This one was available, and once I decided on it, it felt right. Even though I don't live there anymore, Timberhaven will always be home to me."

"Did you ever, when you were younger, consider working for the sawmill?"

"Not really."

Melinda cocked her head. "I would think that having such a demanding job would make it difficult to get away."

"Of course, but I have a life, too." Without any prompting, he turned at the fork in the road that would take them to Holly Pointe. "And this trip wasn't really a vacation. I was going because of the wedding."

"Can you work from anywhere?"

"Conceivably," Jack admitted. "Especially now that I've built my team. The only thing is, being in the city gives me greater access to investors."

"Do you think you'll ever move back to Timberhaven?"

"Hard to say."

Melinda understood. Small-town life wasn't for everyone. Sometimes she wasn't sure it was for her. Other times, she couldn't imagine living anywhere but Holly Pointe. She settled back into the seat and sipped her very delicious latte.

Jack hadn't balked at her request to swing through a coffee drive-through attached to a convenience store in the last town on their way to Holly Pointe.

She'd planned to stick to only a drink, but when he'd ordered two doughnuts and offered her one, well, what could she do but eat it?

The doughnut might be history, but the latte remained. Her lips curved, and she took another sip.

"What about you? Have you always lived in Holly Pointe?"

For a second, Melinda found herself lost in a sugar-induced fog, then realized he'd asked a question.

"I went away to college, then took a marketing job in Burlington." Melinda thought back to when she'd decided to move back to Holly Pointe. "When my mother started having issues with her knee, I moved home to help out. Thankfully, I secured another position, one that allowed me to work remote."

"Will your mom ever be healed enough to be on her own?"

"She had a total knee replacement this past summer." Melinda smiled, recalling her mother's joy when the physical therapist had told her she'd "graduated."

"Her knee is stronger than it has been in years."

Jack inclined his head. "Do you have other family nearby?"

"It's just my brother and me, but he's a local contractor and busy. He's also a single father, so he doesn't have much free time." Realizing how that sounded, Melinda hurriedly added, "Derek helped out a lot after my mom had surgery, as did his daughter, Camryn."

"Would you ever consider moving back to Burlington?"

"No reason now. I was laid off last month."

"I'm sorry to hear that."

Melinda lifted a shoulder, let it drop.

"So, even though you didn't know it at the time, you were coming home to stay."

"It appears so." Melinda took another sip of her latte and considered the life she had now compared to the one in Burlington. "I have lifelong friends here and my family. The people who live in Holly Pointe are amazing, and at this time of year, it's magical."

"I remember coming here during the Christmas season at least once or twice when I was growing up. I don't recall much about it."

"Even if you did, I think you'd be surprised by how much it has changed. The community is constantly searching for new ways to enhance the Christmas experience."

"I can see that. More tourists equal more money in their pockets."

Spoken, Melinda thought, like a true finance person.

"That's some of it, sure, but it's more than that." Melinda struggled to put into words the community feel. "Several years back, Holly Pointe was voted the Capital of Christmas Kindness. Most of the locals truly embrace the holiday spirit and want to share that with visitors."

"Perhaps I'll be able to see that spirit in action for myself."

"If you're interested, I'd be happy to give you a quick tour when we get there." Melinda's lips quirked upward. "Maybe while we're clomping around in the snow, we can pretend we're walking the beach in Mexico."

CHAPTER SEVEN

Melinda texted Lucy and Kate the second the car crossed into the Holly Pointe town limits.

Let's catch up over breakfast tomorrow, Lucy texted back. *We could check out Sugarplums. Please say you'll come.*

Sugarplum's. One more new café to compete with Rosie's. Melinda didn't want to give business to a competitor, but she knew how it would go if they met at Rosie's. Plus, she was curious about the new café.

Perfect time to catch up. Kate's text came on the heels of Lucy's. *See you both at 8?*

I'll be there, Melinda promised and found herself smiling.

Jack slowed the car as they reached Main Street.

Fresh snow blanketed the trees and bushes, but the streets and sidewalks were clear, and the merchants were open for business.

Melinda gestured with one hand toward the diner. "That's my mom's café."

"Rosie's Diner," he said, reading the name on the vintage sign. "Looks nice."

It looked festive, Melinda acknowledged, with its colored lights and window decals, but also in need of some sprucing up.

She recalled Generous Bites in Clatonia with its brightly colored door and eclectic menu. "The food is good."

Even though she was well aware of all the improvements needed, she would not diss her mother's business.

"I'm betting it's better than good." Jack smiled. "You don't stay in the restaurant business for over twenty-five years if you don't offer stellar food and service."

"Very true," Melinda agreed. "Would you prefer to drive around and see the sights or walk, at least the downtown area?"

"After being in the car all these hours, I'm surprised you have to ask."

Melinda smiled. "I was thinking more of the cold."

Jack gaze shifted to the dash. "It's twenty-nine. Practically a heat wave."

"How could I forget you're from this part of the country?" Melinda chuckled and pointed. "There's a parking spot."

When she got out of the car, Melinda realized that, with little wind and lots of sunshine, it did feel balmy. Still, she found herself wishing for a heavier coat.

After glancing down the street in the direction of the diner, Jack turned to her. "Do you want to stop in and let your mother know you made it home safely?"

Melinda chuckled. "No rush. She likely thinks I'm in Mexico."

"Oh." Confusion blanketed Jack's face. "I thought you texted her."

"There was no reason. She couldn't have left the diner to come and get me. Besides, she's busy with Carl."

"Who's Carl?"

"I guess you could say Carl is her boyfriend." Melinda paused, the word awkward on her tongue. "My mother is sixty-three. Talking about her and using the word 'boyfriend' in the same sentence is decidedly odd."

"Do you like him?"

Melinda offered a noncommittal shrug. "He's a clown."

Jack snorted. "I guess that's a no, then."

"Not at all." Melinda shook her head. "I mean he's literally a clown. He visits hospitalized kids and does magic tricks and makes balloon animals."

"You're kidding."

"I never kid about clowns," Melinda told him quite seriously.

Jack laughed. "He sounds like a pretty good guy if he spends his time doing that."

Melinda nodded. "He makes my mom laugh. She's never been much for dating, and she seems happy enough with him. At least for now."

Before Jack could respond, Melinda gestured to Memory Lane, the antique store sitting across the street from Rosie's Diner. "Memory Lane has been here for as long as I can remember. They have a bit of everything, but specialize in vintage Christmas ornaments, children's toys and holiday memorabilia. The stock changes constantly, so it's always fun to wander around and see what's new."

"Let's do it."

"Do what?"

"Wander around and see what's inside." He cocked his head. "Unless you're in a hurry?"

"Not in a hurry." She stepped to the door of the shop. "My calendar for the rest of the day happens to be completely open."

"What a coincidence." Jack smiled. "So is mine."

Melinda reached for the brass door handle, but Jack was faster, reaching around her to pull it open.

He stepped back. "After you."

The shop smelled faintly of pine, likely from the large fir decorated with the antique ornaments she'd mentioned. The pleasant scent mingled with the cinnamon sticks tied with ribbons and had Melinda smiling as she stepped farther into the shop.

"Melinda." Douglas James, portly with a shock of white hair, stepped from behind the counter, a big smile on his face. "This is a surprise. I swear your mother told me you'd be in Mexico this Christmas."

"That was the plan." Melinda offered Doug, a high school classmate of her mother's, a rueful smile. "A computer snafu affecting the airlines squelched my trip to the sunny south."

"I'm sorry to hear that." The man's pale blue eyes behind silver wire-rimmed spectacles shifted to Jack. He stuck out a hand. "I don't believe we've met. I'm Doug James, owner of this fine establishment."

"Jack McPherson." Jack gave the man's hand a shake, then reaching over, he picked up a *Stars Wars* action figure. "I haven't seen one of these since I was a kid."

"They're very popular. This one won't last long. Most—"

"Doug." The feminine voice came from the back of the store. "I want this snow globe, but it's too high up. I'm afraid if I try to get it myself, I'll drop it."

"On my way," Doug called out, then turned back to Melinda and Jack for just a second. "Nice seeing you both."

"Seen enough?" Melinda asked.

Jack nodded, but continued to gaze at Luke Skywalker in his iconic X-wing pilot gear.

"Are you a *Star Wars* fan?"

"Big-time." Jack set the figure down. "My brother and I had them all. We shared them."

"Shared?"

"My father was big on cooperation, not competition." Jack's eyes took on a faraway look. "We're close in age and tended to like the same things."

"Is this the brother who is getting married?"

Jack nodded.

"Are you still close?"

"We were until—" He frowned. "What about your dad?"

Melinda blinked. "What about him?"

"You haven't mentioned him."

An older couple Melinda didn't know held the door for them on their way out before stepping inside the store.

"Does he live in Holly Pointe?" Jack asked when they were on the sidewalk.

"He died shortly after I was born. My mom remarried when I was in grade school, but they divorced a long time ago."

"She's been alone ever since."

There was a question there.

"That's how she likes it." Melinda shrugged. "I mean, I thought that was how she liked it. Carl may prove me wrong."

They continued down the street, strolling side by side past shop windows encircled in twinkling lights while Christmas banners hanging from the antique street poles lining Main Street fluttered in the breeze.

Carolers dressed in period apparel sang to shoppers crowding the sidewalks while, at the far end of the street, the lights on the town's tree brightened the night sky.

Melinda slowed to a stop in front of a bookstore, its front window encased in fairy lights.

"Like Memory Lane, Yule Books is locally owned, though it has changed ownership several times."

"Is local ownership important here?"

"I think it is." Melinda's voice softened. "It's one of the things I love most about Holly Pointe. Most of the business owners have grown up here and feel a connection to the community. They're not just here to make money off of tourists."

When Melinda started to walk on, Jack stopped her with a hand on her arm.

"Since neither of us is in a hurry, let's check it out."

"Sure, I've got time." Not time to wander into every store, but she had a few minutes to spare.

They strolled in and out of the shop's aisles. Jack perused the nonfiction area, then brought a hardback of *Billion Dollar Whale* to the counter.

The female, college-age clerk, another person Melinda didn't recognize, glanced at the front of the book and read the subtitle aloud. "'The man who fooled Wall Street.'"

She looked up and smiled warmly at Jack as she rang up the purchase. "I'm guessing this isn't about a whale."

Jack only chuckled and handed her a credit card.

"Are you interested in finance?" the clerk asked.

"I am. What about you?" Jack asked, sounding genuinely interested.

"I'm going to be a teacher." The clerk handed him a sack with the book tucked inside.

"I bet you'll make a great one." Jack then turned to Melinda. "Ready?"

Once outside the shop, Melinda considered where to take him next as a gust of wind sliced through her as if her light jacket didn't exist. Hunching her shoulders against the cold, she swiveled to ask what he was interested in seeing, but she found him staring.

When his gaze lingered on her lips for half a heartbeat, blood surged through Melinda's veins like an awakened river.

For a second, she thought he might kiss her.

For a second, she thought she might let him.

Then Jack pointed to Jingle Shells. "What about this place?"

Melinda forced a smile. "It's a relatively new restaurant and extremely popular. All the dishes have fun names, like Frosty the Sno-Manicotti and Fa-La-La-Lasagna. The interior has a trendy vibe." Melinda's gaze lingered on the number of customers standing in line waiting to be seated. "The thing is, the owners are from out of state and only decided to open the café after we were dubbed the Capital of Christmas Kindness. Everything they do is a gimmick."

A look of understanding filled Jack's eyes. "When you

mentioned the diner to me, you said your mom is struggling. Are you going to speak with her again about possible changes?"

"She doesn't want to hear anything like that from me." Melinda gave a humorless laugh. "Mom might talk about wanting to make a change from time to time, but in the end, she never makes a move."

"Would you be interested in taking over the diner?"

"I would never want to take something from my mom. It's her dream. I want her to keep her dream."

Jack opened his mouth, then shut it, apparently reconsidering whatever he'd been about to say.

This gave Melinda the opening she'd been hoping for. "How about we go back to the car and I can show you the rest of the town from the comfort of a space that has a heater set on high?"

"Sounds like a plan."

When his gaze landed on her once again, she felt a blast of heat. That warmth sustained her all the way to the car.

Once in the car, they drove by Landers Tree Farm, then past the hill everyone used for sledding. Though it wasn't yet dark, the lights were already on, and the fresh snow on the ground appeared to have brought out the kids.

"Looks like a popular place."

"It's where everyone goes to sled. They also have snow bowling competitions and races." Melinda pointed. "Turn right at the next intersection."

She directed him to Spring Lake, which sat at the edge of town and where two middle-school-age teams currently battled for hockey supremacy. To her surprise, the lights had been turned on here as well. "Pond hockey is huge here."

"It's big in Timberhaven as well."

"Do you play?"

"Everyone plays."

"Dustin Bellamy comes to Holly Pointe every Christmas with his wife and their twin boys. While he's here, Dustin teaches hockey classes for beginners and coaches the older kids."

Surprise skittered across Jack's face, and she saw he recognized Dustin's name. "Having a former NHL MVP has to be a draw."

"Truer words." Melinda smiled. "Now for the town's crowning glory. Turn left at the next intersection, then right."

The Barns at Grace Hollow soon came into view, lighting up the night sky with a golden glow. Nestled between tall pines, the two barns stood tall and majestic. Constructed of reclaimed lumber, stone and steel, they drew the eye.

"Wow." Jack slanted a glance at her. "Impressive."

She smiled, pleased he found the Barns as amazing as she did.

"The Barns at Grace Hollow." Jack read the sign at the end of the long drive. "What are they? There are certainly a lot of cars in the lot."

"Events venue," Melinda explained. "The style is very similar to the Big Sky Barn in Texas. The smaller of the two has lots of gorgeous stained glass. It's often used for weddings, but can be used for smaller events like anniversary parties, retirement parties, graduations…stuff like that."

"The big one appears to be where all the action is." After finding a place to park in the lot, Jack cut the engine. "Do you have any idea what's going on inside?"

Melinda smiled. With Lucy being one of her besties, she knew everything that went on in the Barns. "Holiday Marketplace. It runs every day in December. It's really cool. There are dozens of vendors selling everything from outfits for your favorite pet to emu oil."

"Emu oil?" Jack arched a skeptical brow. "You're making that up."

Laughter bubbled up inside Melinda and spilled out. "God's truth."

Jack shook his head. "Something for everyone."

Melinda paused, considered. Maybe she had more time to spend with him after all. "Want to go inside?"

He grinned. "I thought you'd never ask."

CHAPTER EIGHT

Jack glanced around the cavernous interior of the Big Barn. Aisle after aisle sported vendor booths selling everything from yarn made from pet hair to handmade candles sporting names like Peppermint Swirl, Sugar Cookie Bliss and, his favorite, Cozy Fireplace.

"I can't believe you bought that candle." Melinda teased when they stepped away from the booth and began to stroll down the next aisle.

He lifted the sack and grinned. "Where else can I find a portable Cozy Fireplace?"

"Melinda."

The woman, dressed all in black with a mass of blonde hair held back from her face with a sparkly band, threw her arms around Melinda.

Jack watched with interest as the two talked at once.

Then Melinda turned and gestured for him to step closer. "Lucy, this is Jack McPherson."

This, he surmised, was the Lucy who'd kept Melinda under close surveillance during the drive to Holly Pointe.

He offered her a warm smile. "It's a pleasure to put a face with a name."

Lucy's assessing gaze lingered on him for a moment, then she smiled. "Thank you for bringing her home safely."

"She was good company."

"Yes," Lucy slanted a glance at Melinda, "yes, she is."

Then she returned her attention back to Jack. "What do you think of the Barns?"

"So far I've only been in this one, but it's incredible."

From the way her lips curved, his response appeared to please her. She turned to Melinda. "You should show him the Baby Barn."

Jack cocked his head. "Baby Barn?"

"Not real babies." Lucy laughed. "It's what everyone calls the smaller barn."

"It was lit up." Melinda shot her friend a quizzical look. "I thought there was probably an event going on."

"Not tonight. The staff is getting it ready for tomorrow night's Ugly Sweater Mixer."

Understanding flashed in Melinda's eyes. "I forgot about the mixer."

"This is the first year for it," Melinda told him before her attention returned to Lucy. "Have you seen a good response?"

"More tickets sold than I anticipated, which makes me happy." Lucy smiled. "People can still buy tickets at the door. And, by the number of ugly sweaters that Trudy has sold in her Festive Frump booth, I'm anticipating a large turnout."

"I wondered why there were so many people lined up to buy ugly sweaters." Jack shook his head. "Some of those sweaters are really ugly."

"The uglier the better is what I say." Lucy then shifted toward Melinda. "You're coming, aren't you? I mean, now that you're back in town, there shouldn't be anything stopping you."

"I'll definitely be there," Melinda assured her friend.

"Do we need to stop back at the Festive Frump booth?" Just saying the name made Jack smile.

Melinda inclined her head and shot him a questioning glance.

"So you can pick up your ugly sweater for tomorrow night," he explained.

She waved a dismissive hand. "I have several."

He arched an eyebrow. "You collect ugly sweaters?"

"In a manner of speaking. My brother gives me one every Christmas." Though she rolled her eyes, Jack saw the fondness for her sibling reflected in her hazel depths. "They're quality sweaters, but they are ugly."

"They really are." Lucy shook her head and chuckled. "My favorite is the one your brother gave you a couple of years ago."

"Which one was that?" Melinda asked. "They all blur together."

"The Rockin' Around the Christmas Tree one with the reindeer sporting an oversized pair of sunglasses and a Santa hat?" Lucy paused, then added, "If I'm remembering correctly, the reindeer's eyes sparkle with sequins."

"Don't forget the glittering snowflakes, twinkling stars and dangling ornaments." Melinda shook her head. "My brother sure knows how to pick 'em."

"Sounds festive," Jack said, trying not to smile.

"It's actually quite cute. It…" Lucy paused when the walkie-talkie on her hip squawked.

Jack had trouble making out the words, but Lucy appeared to understand what was being said.

"Duty calls." Shooting them an apologetic smile, she gave Melinda another fierce hug. "I'm so glad you're back."

Once she released Melinda, Lucy turned to him. "Thanks again for bringing her home. Oh, and if you have time, you two should stop over and inspect the Baby Barn. The decorations are amazing."

She hurried off then, her brows pulled together in concentration as she made a call on her phone.

"Does she manage this venue?" Jack asked, trying to put the pieces together.

"You could say that." Melinda smiled. "She's the owner."

~

When Melinda offered to show Jack the smaller barn, she wasn't sure he'd be interested. Though there was certainly a good amount of daylight left, she hated the thought of him driving along wooded roadways after dark.

Despite her worry, she had to admit she was pleased when he said he'd like to take a look at the decorations.

"I can't imagine how you'd decorate for an ugly-sweater event," he admitted as they crossed through the enclosed walkway connecting the two venues.

"If I know Lucy, it's going to be spectacular." Melinda quickened her steps to greet an older woman with tight gray curls who stood watch outside the interior entrance to the smaller barn. "Eileen, it's so good to see you. I didn't know you worked here."

"Just helping Lucy during December. I've discovered retirement isn't all it's cracked up to be." Eileen offered a rueful smile. "I missed the daily contact with people, especially those I don't know. Like this handsome gentleman at your side."

Melinda turned to Jack then and made short work of introducing him. Instead of going into detail, she simply said he was a friend from New Hampshire. "For as long as I can remember, Eileen oversaw the Holly Pointe cabins."

"The ones we passed leading out of town?"

Jack might have glanced at Melinda for confirmation, but it was Eileen who responded.

"Those are the ones." Eileen glanced down and flicked a piece of lint from her shirt. When she looked up again, her carefully composed expression gave nothing away. "The previous owner sold to Schaefer Brothers out of Boston. They wanted to make a lot of changes, and I, well, I thought it was a good time to go."

Sympathy blanketed Jack's face. "That had to be a difficult decision."

"It helped that Kate Sullivan took over for me."

"My friend Kate," Melinda told Jack.

"Yes, those two have been good friends for eons. Always together at all the holiday celebrations." Eileen paused, and her brows pulled together in puzzlement. "Why did I think you were in Mexico?"

"Long story." Melinda kept her tone light. "Jack and I thought we'd take a look at the decorations for the party tomorrow. Lucy told us it would be okay."

"I believe they just finished, or maybe are just finishing up." Eileen pushed a button on the wall that opened the door leading to the barn. "Prepare to smile."

Moments later, Melinda and Jack gazed in disbelief at the scene spread before them. For a couple of seconds, Melinda simply stared, unsure how to respond.

Jack finally cleared his throat. "I've been to lots of parties, but have never been to one with such, ah, eye-catching decorations."

"They definitely catch the eye. It's difficult to look away." Melinda glanced up to the garland strung across the walls and around the entrance. Made out of mini ugly Christmas sweaters attached by a red ribbon with green polka dots, the sight had her smiling.

"The tacky Christmas lights are my favorite," Jack said with utmost seriousness, his gaze lingering on the colorful string lights with mismatched and oversized bulbs strung around the bar area and flashing.

Melinda gestured to an area labeled DIY Ugly Sweater Photo Booth. The backdrop was a fabric of bright and clashing colors, and a sign encouraged participants to "Strike an Ugly Pose."

"I predict that's going to be a big hit."

"I'd say that's a definite." Jack studied her for a long moment. "You were right."

"I'm right about a lot of things." She offered him a cheeky smile. "Which right are you referring to?"

"This town really does have a lot to offer over the holidays."

"Oh, Jack." Melinda placed a hand on his arm. "You ain't seen nothing yet."

~

"There it is. The Candy Cane Christmas House." Melinda's hand swept out as if she tried to encompass the entire spectacle laid out before them.

Jack stared at the mammoth three-story Victorian house. It had turrets that rose to the clouds and towers so tall that even Rapunzel's hair couldn't have reached the ground. Added to all that were enough lights blazing to take down an entire city's electrical grid.

"Quick," Melinda prompted. "First impression."

The one word that came immediately to mind fell from Jack's lips like the white icicle lights hanging from the eaves. "Bright."

Melinda chuckled and reached for the handle of her car door. "Wait until you see the inside."

Once they'd left the Barns at Grace Hollow, Melinda had directed him here. She hadn't told him where they were going or what they would see, only that she was certain he would find it unforgettable.

She'd been right. Again.

Instead of immediately heading to the front door, they stopped on the sidewalk.

Lighted candy canes shone their brightness on both sides of the path leading to the porch. The greenery that wrapped around the porch railings contained a plethora of red bows along with more lights.

He turned to Melinda. "What is this place?"

"Only one of the busiest spots in Holly Pointe during the holidays." She took his arm as they strode down the walkway to the porch. "Locals and tourists come here to bake cookies together, to make ornaments and wrap gifts for soldiers and kids whose families need a little help. There are classes on how to make candy, wreaths and gingerbread houses. Santa comes here on a regular basis to pose with kids of all ages for pictures with the house as a backdrop. Seniors can be found here several nights a week in December playing Christmas bingo."

By the time she finished recounting all that went on under the massive roof, Jack's head swam. Behind the awe and admiration for anyone bold enough to take on such an adventurous venture, his financial side clicked on. "How is all of this financed? The electric bill has to be huge, and the supplies for all the classes would add up."

Melinda paused when they reached the porch and inclined her head, her brows furrowed in thought. "I know that people pay for the classes and that Ginny and Mary, who do most of the teaching, do it out of love for the community and don't expect to be reimbursed. I believe they receive money under some sort of dedicated community funds in the budget. If Sam were here, he could probably answer your questions."

"Sam?"

"Sam Johnson. He's the city administrator, and he and his wife are friends of mine." Melinda shrugged. "I'd say you could ask him yourself when you see him, but since you're leaving, the funding will remain an unsolved mystery."

Melinda reached for the door handle, but Jack placed a hand on her arm.

"No need to go inside." Jack kept his voice low. "If they have a class or something, we'll be interrupting."

"No worries." She flashed a bright smile and opened the door. "If there is something going on, we'll simply join in on the fun."

CHAPTER NINE

Ten minutes later, Melinda sat beside Jack at a large rectangular table in the front parlor of the Candy Cane Christmas House. An assortment of gingerbread pieces were now laid out on the cake board in front of them.

There were more lights in here, the brightest of them on the oversized Christmas tree that reached all the way to the ceiling. Decorated with an abundance of glittery ornaments and twinkling lights, it definitely drew the eye.

The mantel of the fireplace boasted elaborately designed greenery with ribbons, sparkling ornaments and more lights.

"Thoughts on how to begin?"

Melinda's question appeared to pull Jack's attention back from the sparkling crown-shaped tree topper encrusted with faux diamonds, gemstones and glitter that Mary Pierson—the owner and proprietress—had pointed out was new this year.

His gaze dropped to study the pieces laid out before them. Then he glanced back at Melinda. "When the woman said someone had canceled and there was an extra gingerbread house to decorate, I thought the house itself would come already assembled."

He gestured with one hand to the others at the table who'd already begun decorating their houses.

Melinda picked up a piece of the dense cake. "More fun for us. This way, we get to decide on the design and layout of our house."

Studying the piece in her hand, Melinda cocked her head. "There are any number of layouts we could go with other than classic cottage, but we're getting a later start than the others, so I suggest we stick to the basic design."

"I agree," Jack said, "but just out of curiosity, what are some other designs?"

"Well." Melinda brought a finger to her lips and thought. "There's a candy castle. We would build it with turrets, towers and drawbridges. Or a treehouse, where the house is nestled within the branches of a gingerbread tree. Or a candy shop, where we'd fill the walls inside with colorful candies, lollipops and candy canes. Or the festive chalet, where—"

"Stop." Jack held up a hand. "Let's stick with the classic cottage."

"Are you sure you have time for this?" While Melinda had observed firsthand that Jack was an excellent driver, darkness wasn't far off. "I mean, Mary didn't give us much choice, and by the time this sets up and we finish, it'll be dark. I don't know what the roads are like where you're headed, but here they're snow-packed and could be icy—"

The warmth of Jack's hand closing over hers had Melinda's thoughts stuttering.

His blue eyes met hers and held. "I wouldn't have agreed if I hadn't wanted to do it with you. As far as the drive, I'm not worried."

If he wasn't worried, she wouldn't be either.

A flush of pleasure had her smiling as she picked up a piece of gingerbread. "This is going to be so much fun."

The excitement that wove its way through Melinda's words

like a pretty ribbon was genuine. How long had it been since she'd taken time to do something like this?

With all the needed supplies in front of them, including royal icing acting as glue to hold the gingerbread pieces together, it didn't take much time for them to have the walls and roof in place.

"I brought you a couple of items to help that royal icing harden more quickly." Mary set a tiny fan on the table, then handed Jack a hair dryer. "You'll want to keep this on cool."

"Thanks, Mary." Melinda knew that Ginny Blain normally handled the gingerbread stuff, but she was in New York with Faith, Graham and the girls. "How are you holding up without Ginny?"

Mary's sweet smile, when combined with her lithe frame, white hair and pale blue eyes, gave her an ethereal appearance. "I'm happy she can spend this time with Faith and Graham. I only wish I could be there with them."

"I texted Faith a couple of days ago," Melinda told her. "No baby yet."

"You'd have heard." Mary rested a hand on Melinda's shoulder. "You're one of the first friends she'll call."

"He's due at any time." Melinda smiled, thinking how excited Graham and Faith, as well as the twins, were about the new baby.

"I said to Ginny, wouldn't it be wonderful if he came on Christmas? You know, it's going to be a full moon."

"Christmas Moon," Melinda murmured. "The first time that's happened in thirty years."

"Christmas Moon?" Though he kept the dryer aimed at the icing, Jack shifted his gaze to them.

"A full moon on Christmas," Mary explained. "It symbolizes new beginnings."

"Oh, Mary," the woman at the other end of the table called out, "when you have time, could you come over here? We have a problem."

"Be right there," Mary called, then placed a hand on Melinda's shoulder. "Don't forget, your cottage walls and roof are weak. Normally, we like to have those pieces set up overnight, or at least for a couple of hours before you begin to decorate. Using the fan and the hair dryer is an old trick to help it set up more quickly, but be very gentle when you decorate."

Working in tandem, Melinda and Jack added gumdrops and tiny candy canes to the exterior, being careful not to put too much pressure on the structure.

Melinda took the frosting bag. In her head, she could already see the intricate design she planned to create on the front of the house. She turned to Jack. "When you use a frosting bag, it's important to apply firm, even pressure, but you don't want to squeeze it too hard or—"

Without warning, the bag exploded in a frosting explosion, covering part of Jack's face and most of his shirtfront.

Conversation ceased at the table.

Melinda inhaled sharply.

Appearing not at all disturbed, Jack wiped frosting off his face with the side of his finger, then stuck it into his mouth. "Hmm, tasty."

"I'm so sorry." Frantically, Melinda looked around on the table for a clean cloth. Finding none, she started to rise when she felt his hand on her arm.

"I'm fine. Really. Let's keep going."

They kept going.

Mary brought him a cloth to remove the icing from his face, and he was able to get most of it off his shirt.

The house was nearly complete and looking pretty darned good, but... "It needs something else."

Jack studied the structure, then at the supplies set out on the table. "What about sprinkles? They'd add a bit more color to the roof."

"Great idea." She gestured to the sprinkles. "You get the honors."

Picking up the container, Jack began enthusiastically shaking it. Brightly colored pieces fell like snow over the top of the house.

"Just a little more," Melinda suggested.

Jack gave the container an enthusiastic final shake. The lid popped off, resulting in an avalanche of colorful sprinkles.

The weight of the candy proved more than the weakened structure could handle. The cottage collapsed in on itself.

Melinda couldn't help it. She burst into laughter.

Jack's laughter came just as quickly. "Well, that was fun."

The thing was, Melinda thought as they said their good-byes a half hour later, it had been fun. In fact, she couldn't recall the last time she'd enjoyed a date so much.

Date? No, she reminded herself as she got into the small car, this wasn't a date, just her showing Jack around town.

Then why couldn't she keep from wondering if there was going to be a good-night kiss at the end of the evening?

By the time Jack pulled up in front of Melinda's house and unloaded her luggage from the trunk, he lingered on the sidewalk, reluctant to say good-bye. Once he left, it would likely be the last time he'd see her. "Thanks again for the tour."

"You're very welcome."

"I'm sorry about the implosion." Still, he couldn't help but smile, remembering how they'd enjoyed a treat of gumdrops and sprinkles off mangled gingerbread.

"I'm not." Melinda's lips curved. "It added a dash of excitement to the evening."

"More than a dash." Jack smiled back at her. "It's not often you completely demolish a gingerbread house."

"If we're not careful, Santa is going to put lumps of coal in our stockings this year."

Jack laughed. "That'd be disappointing and messy."

"I guess it would." Melinda's eyes looked golden in the street-light's glow. "If you'd been around longer, I'd have introduced you to Kenny Douglas, our resident Santa. I can't imagine him putting a piece of coal in anyone's stocking, no matter how well-deserved. He and his wife run the Busy Bean Coffee & Tea Shop...and he is the perfect Santa. Not only does he look the part with the long white beard, but he's the nicest, kindest man you'll ever meet. He—"

While she continued to tell him about Kenny and the special Santa activities in Holly Pointe, Jack murmured encouraging sounds and tossed out an occasional "Oh, really?" in order to keep her talking.

He liked the way her eyes lit up and her animated expression as she told him about the Snowman Parade and how Kenny, dressed as Santa, arrived on a sleigh pulled by actual reindeer.

"Santa used to arrive in Holly Pointe the weekend after Thanksgiving, but since so many people have family in town for Thanksgiving, now he comes that weekend and appears at the Snowman Parade."

"Makes sense." Jack had heard before how Holly Pointe did Christmas up right. Only now was he beginning to understand what that meant. "So, even though some times are set in stone, you're still flexible."

"Yes, but we try to be aware that some people plan their trips here around specific activities. Which means we wouldn't want to change the date of the Snowman Parade." Melinda's gaze grew thoughtful as she appeared to be thinking of other examples. "Normally, the Mistletoe Ball is held the weekend before Christmas. This year, it's being held on Christmas Day—in the evening, of course."

"Mistletoe Ball?"

"It's our biggest holiday event and is held at Grace Hollow. Ninety percent of the profits are donated to the University of Vermont Cancer Center. Ten percent stays in Holly Pointe to address local health care needs."

"While giving so much to charity is admirable, that means that Lucy makes nothing for hosting the event?"

"She could charge for the event space, sure, but that would mean less money for the cancer center. The food vendors and others are paid. Once their costs are taken out, that's the amount that is donated."

Jack nodded. "Makes sense."

"The decision to go with an Ugly Sweater Mixer was a calculated one. It gives those who may not be able to stay for the Mistletoe Ball on Christmas the chance to enjoy a holiday party in Holly Pointe."

"How do you know so much about all of this?"

"I've lived here all my life, remember?" She smiled. "I also serve on a number of planning committees."

A momentary silence filled the air between them, something he thought of as a kind of watchful waiting. As if both of them were deciding next steps.

For once, Jack, who prided himself on always being three steps ahead of everyone else, found himself unsure and off-balanced.

"Well, I suppose this is good-bye." Melinda assumed he would just drive off once he'd set her luggage at her feet.

She didn't want him to leave, which she knew was why she'd rattled on and on when she should have been encouraging him to get on the road.

She wasn't sure what to think when he took her hands in his, and she discovered she couldn't tear her gaze from his mesmerizing blue eyes.

"Thank you for the tour."

With her eyes still fixed on his, Melinda cleared her throat. "Thanks again for driving me home."

Then it struck her. She hadn't paid him for gas. The knowledge broke the web that tethered them together. Pulling her hands from his, she reached into the bag slung over her shoulder and pulled a few bills from her wallet. "I'm sorry, I forgot about the gas money."

His warm hand closed over the one she extended with the cash. "I don't want your money. But I appreciate the offer."

Jack stood close now, so close she could see the gold flecks in his blue eyes.

"Are you sure?"

"I'm positive." His tone left no room for doubt.

Though she knew she was behaving like a lovestruck teen, she couldn't seem to stop herself. "Y-you should come back sometime, stay a few days."

A tiny smile lifted his lips. Without shifting his gaze, he brushed a strand of hair back from her face with a gentle finger. "I just may do that."

His voice, that deep husky rumble, did strange things to her insides. The same way it had all evening.

"If you do, be sure and stay through Christmas. That way, you can really see what makes Holly Pointe special." Her heart began an erratic rhythm. "That's when you get the magic."

Jack smiled, more fully this time.

Melinda wasn't sure what got into her. Maybe it was knowing this might be the last time she'd ever see him. If she didn't do it now, she'd always wonder what it would have been like.

Giving in to desire, Melinda leaned forward and kissed him on the mouth. His lips were warm, and he tasted deliciously sweet, like a mixture of candy canes and gumdrops.

When his arms stole around her, it felt so natural to wrap her arms around him.

Melinda couldn't say how long they stood there with their arms wrapped around each other, kissing.

She knew only that when she finally was waving good-bye to him from her porch, she realized that forty-eight hours with him had not been nearly long enough.

CHAPTER TEN

That night, Melinda found her dreams filled with thoughts of Jack. Only they weren't in Holly Pointe—they were in Mexico, enjoying sun and sand. She woke alone to snow falling and a sense of sadness.

She'd wanted that step away from reality, had really needed it. Not simply because a visit to a beach was always nice, but the loss of her online marketing job had meant she'd recently been spending more time at the diner.

She loved the café and all of the customers, both the familiar ones and the ones in town for the holiday. What she didn't love, and what had really started to chafe, was her mother's resistance to change and Melinda's own lack of purpose.

Like she'd told Jack, she'd brought up possible additions to the menu only to get those shot down.

The same thing had happened when she had spent hours looking at various diner designs online. Melinda had come up with several possible changes for the exterior of Rosie's Diner. Ones that would have brought the diner into the twenty-first century and wouldn't have taken much capital investment. Her mother's response to all her suggestions had been lukewarm at best.

While she could understand her mother wanting to preserve the feel of the diner, they had to appeal to a whole new generation of customers. Customers who had, more and more, been frequenting other cafés and restaurants in town.

Last summer, Melinda had thought she was getting somewhere. Her mother had sat down and gone through the possibilities Melinda had put together. Derek had tossed in his support for the idea, saying he'd do the renovation work for just the cost of materials.

For several days in August, Melinda had thought her mother might agree. Then Rosie had started spending even more time with Carl and had suddenly been too busy to consider the options. Melinda had pressed, but her mother had told her to drop it. There would be no changes.

When Rosie had added that Carl loved the diner just the way it was, Melinda had been forced to grit her teeth to keep from saying Carl was simply the man Rosie had been dating since the beginning of the summer. He didn't have a vote.

Only then had Melinda realized that neither did she.

Heaving a resigned sigh, Melinda did what she always did when facing any obstacle—she pushed forward. Which meant getting dressed for breakfast with friends.

Since she'd slept in, she got herself together in record time. Melinda had to admit that it felt strange that they'd be meeting at Sugarplum's. When she'd called her mother last night to tell her she was back, she'd mentioned she was meeting Lucy and Kate for breakfast.

Telling her mother that they were meeting somewhere other than Rosie's...well, that conversation had gone about as she'd expected.

Now, sitting at a white lacquer table with the sun shining

through the windows of Sugarplum's, she felt herself begin to relax.

The large windows provided glimpses of the snowy landscape outside. The frosty patterns on the glass added a touch of whimsy, while the vinyl clings, well, unlike Rosie's elves doing a conga line, these were delicate, hand-painted snowflakes.

Here, no smell of frying food and strong coffee greeted you when you walked through the door. Instead, the air in Sugarplum's was filled with the comforting aroma of freshly baked gingerbread, cinnamon and spiced cider.

As she inhaled deeply, Melinda wondered if the scent was piped in, or if those were actual smells from the kitchen.

"That tree is amazing." Lucy took a sip of her Eggnog Latte and studied the large fir adorned with an array of whimsical ornaments and shimmering tinsel.

"It makes the one in my cabin look positively tacky." Kate chuckled.

"Your tree is gorgeous." Melinda reached over and squeezed Kate's hand.

Assuming she'd be out of town for Christmas, Melinda hadn't gotten a tree. Now, seeing how adorable the unicorns, mermaids and dragon ornaments were, she wondered if she should pick up new decorations before putting up a tree in the next few days.

Glancing down at her ceramic coffee mug, hand-thrown by a local artist, Melinda sighed and voiced the comment that her friends were too polite to utter. "I can see why this place is stealing away our customers."

"It definitely rocks the Christmas vibe," Lucy admitted, studying the café with a businesswoman's eye. "I love the specialty lattes and mochas. I'm definitely going to have to come by and try the Cranberry Mocha."

"Their regular coffee is good, too." Kate lifted her mug and took a sip.

"I like the names embroidered on the red aprons, but give me a break. I know that server over there. His name is Ted, not Donner." Melinda watched their server, Merry—and she didn't for one second believe that was the girl's real name—bustle about, a bright smile on her face.

"You're right. A little too cutesy for my taste," Kate agreed.

Melinda's lips quirked upward. "It'd be kind of fun to see our servers wearing ugly Christmas sweaters."

"You could definitely do that," Lucy enthusiastically agreed. "I bet your customers would love it."

"That'd be easy to implement—" Melinda stopped herself. "Forget it. Mom would never go for it."

"I still think it's a fun idea." Lucy set down her cup, her gaze focused on Melinda. "Enough business talk. It's time to move on to more interesting topics."

"Such as?" Melinda could see her friend had something on her mind.

"Tells us all about Mr. Jack McPherson. Don't spare the specifics. While I feel I have a good grasp on him from my research, nothing beats firsthand knowledge."

The mischievous twinkle in Lucy's blue depths made Melinda smile. "What is it with married people, anyway? You all seem to have this fascination with your single friends' lives?"

"I'm not married," Kate interjected without giving Lucy a chance to respond, "and I'm very interested in what went on in that car."

"Don't forget the night they spent together in Wilbur," Lucy reminded her.

"Oh, I haven't forgotten." Kate leaned forward, resting her forearms on the table. "Dish."

"Well, we had hot sex all night long on the floor of this empty attic and—"

The sound of their young server clearing her throat had them turning. Merry's bright smile appeared frozen on her face. "I, ah, just wanted to let you know your food should be out shortly."

"Thanks, Merry." Lucy beamed at the girl, who, after casting one last quick glance at Melinda, backed quickly away.

"Her face." Melinda shook her head and chuckled.

"Gives her something interesting to talk to her friends about." Kate waved a dismissive hand. "Back to the hot sex on the attic floor. Please tell me you at least put down an old sheet or something. Rolling around on a dirty floor isn't that great of a visual."

"If we would have had hot sex, we would have put down a sheet." Melinda cocked her head. "Satisfied?"

"For now." Kate smiled. "Continue."

"The owner of the B&B, which was really more of a private home with a spare room, asked if we wanted to share a bedroom, since they only had one open. Because I knew the two of you would have my head if I slept in the same room with a guy I just met, I got the bed. He got the attic."

"He got the bed in the attic," Lucy clarified and took a long sip of her latte.

"He got the floor." Melinda cast a look at Kate. "They did give him their son's old sleeping bag."

Kate grimaced. "Poor guy."

"He didn't seem to mind." In fact, Melinda recalled, Jack hadn't once complained.

Lucy gave an approving nod. "He's a good sport."

"Yes, I guess he is." Melinda shrugged. "One thing surprised me, though. You'd told me how his family owns Timberhaven Sawmill. Well, the older son of the couple who owns the B&B—who were incredibly sweet, by the way—lives in Timberhaven and is trying to get a job at the sawmill, but apparently can't even get an interview."

Lucy took another long drink of her latte. "I'm sure they get a lot of applicants."

"The thing is, Jack's family owns the sawmill. He could have helped the boy by making one phone call." Melinda frowned, still puzzled that Jack hadn't offered to put in a good word.

"Maybe there's a reason the guy isn't getting an interview, much less being hired." Kate, always the practical one, offered an alternative opinion, likely based on her experience managing a group of cabins at the edge of town. Her job involved not only the financial aspect and overseeing booking, but hiring and supervising the cleaning and maintenance staff. "There might be something in his background that's a red flag."

"The parents say no." Melinda recalled vividly Kent's comments in defense of his son.

"The parents are often the last to know." Lucy shrugged. "I just know, from all the hiring—and firing—that I do at Grace Hollow, that sometimes you do a little digging, and a skeleton pops out."

"A skeleton? It'd be nice if one popped out around Halloween." The impish gleam in Kate's eyes gave her away.

Lucy rolled her eyes.

Melinda laughed. "Okay, so maybe that was the reason Jack didn't offer to help, but he's clearly used to going after and getting what he wants."

"Examples, please." Kate made a come-on gesture with one hand.

Melinda told them about the incident with the rental car and then about him offering the Kastens two hundred dollars to sleep on their floor.

"I don't see a problem." Lucy set down her now-empty latte glass. "In fact, I'm betting if you'd had the money and didn't want to sleep in a car, you'd have done the same."

"Maybe. Probably." After a second, Melinda admitted to herself she would have likely done the same, except she'd have made the Kastens take the cash, even if it was for sleeping on the floor. "It doesn't matter. He's likely in the White Mountains by now."

"Would you like to see him again?" Kate asked.

"I would, but I'm not holding my breath that will happen."

Melinda didn't want to talk about Jack anymore. It only made her miss him. Which was crazy, considering they'd met only forty-eight hours ago.

Shift the focus, Melinda told herself. "I'm super excited about all the events this weekend."

"My ugly sweater is ready to horrify and amuse tonight." Kate relaxed against the back of her chair. "If I'm feeling particularly adventurous, I may even don the hideous Christmas shoes I made. They would be the perfect accompaniment to the sweater."

"What do these hideous shoes of yours look like?" This was the first Melinda had heard of them.

"I call them my Festive Faux Fur Fiasco Shoes." Kate chuckled as if just the name made her smile. "I was bored one night and took a pair of plain canvas shoes and glued faux fur trim around the edges. The fur is in shades of red and green."

"Sounds...interesting." Melinda spoke cautiously.

"They do sound hideous. You should definitely wear them." Lucy gave a decisive nod. "Speaking of tonight, I can't wait to see both of you at the mixer."

"Wouldn't miss it." Melinda glanced at Kate. "Kate agreed to let me tag along with her."

"You two will have lots of fun." Lucy smiled.

"She might go with me." Kate's lips lifted in a slight smile. "But I'm pretty sure I won't be the one driving her home."

Melinda shot her friend a quizzical glance as Merry set down her Sweet Berry Parfait. Layers of creamy Greek yogurt, mixed berries and crunchy granola were garnished with a sprig of fresh mint and a dusting of confectioner's sugar.

"That looks nice and healthy," Lucy said before Kate could clarify her comment. "Unlike this—"

Lucy gestured to the plate holding her Banana Toast—thick slices of artisan bread slathered with creamy Nutella, topped with sliced caramelized bananas and a sprinkle of toasted coconut.

"I think if Goldilocks were rating our breakfasts, she'd say that Melinda's is too healthy, Lucy's is too rich, and mine is just right." Kate lifted her fork and gazed appreciatively at her plate containing a veggie omelet with whole wheat toast and fruit.

"Put that fork down." Melinda pinned Kate with her gaze. "Before you dig in, you need to explain your comment."

"What comment?" Though her expression remained innocent, Kate's lips quirked up enough to let Melinda know she was right to push.

"I'd like to know who you think I'd accept a ride home from tonight, especially since I'm going to the party with you." Melinda waited for some remark about her obviously being open to getting into a car with anyone since she'd accepted a ride from a stranger at an airport.

Lucy looked up, then flicked a tiny bit of Nutella off her red lips with the tip of her tongue. "I was wondering that, too."

"Jack McPherson," was all Kate said before bringing a bite of omelet to her mouth.

"Not possible. He's gone." The realization brought with it another wave of sadness. Melinda really had enjoyed yesterday. "He's probably in his family's cabin in the White Mountains by now."

This time, Kate couldn't hold back her smile. "He's in a cabin all right, but the one I'm thinking of is right here in Holly Pointe."

For a second, the crunchy granola stuck in Melinda's throat. She lifted her coffee and washed it down. "He stayed?"

"He did indeed. He's nice and cozy in Reindeer Rest." This time, Kate smiled full-out. "I hadn't been able to rent RR because we were waiting for a part for the furnace. The thermocouple came in and was installed yesterday. Jack walked into my office just as the furnace guy was leaving. I rented him the cabin through the end of the year."

"I thought you had a waiting list for cancellations." Lucy's brows pulled together. "Shouldn't you have called one of them first?"

"The wait list is at my discretion." Kate shrugged. "I made an executive decision to rent it to him. The way I see it, one good turn deserves another."

"The one good turn being?" Melinda prompted.

Kate smiled. "Jack was nice enough to help Melinda. How could I not help him back?"

CHAPTER ELEVEN

Jack glanced around the cabin he'd moved into and gave a nod of satisfaction. The three-bedroom was larger than he needed, but he liked space, and the rate had been very reasonable. Plus, it had been the only available option.

As Kate had indicated, it came fully furnished, not only with linens and blankets, but a kitchen with all the necessities, including a coffee unit that was decidedly high-tech.

The only thing missing was the food. Melinda had pointed out the market when she'd given him the tour of Holly Pointe highlights. He decided he'd swing by there in the next couple of days.

Not that he planned to buy much. He'd already decided that he would eat most of his meals out. Jack saw that as a win-win. Not only would he be adding money to the coffers of local businesses, he wouldn't have the bother of cooking.

Glancing at his watch, he considered what time it would be at the resort in Mexico where his family was. One hour behind. Not too early to call, and that way he'd have it out of the way.

The way he'd ended the conversation with his mother when they'd last spoken had left him unsettled. She was doing her best to navigate the treacherous waters between the two sons she loved. He admired her for it.

If she would just quit pushing me...

Yet, he knew that dogged determination was part of her personality and the reason she'd been so successful, along with his father, at building the sawmill into the business it was today.

Pulling his phone from his pocket, Jack stared at it, then selected her name from his favorites. He knew regret would just hang over him if he didn't make the call.

"Jack." Relief sounded in his mother's voice. "It's good to hear from you. Where are you?"

"I'm in Holly Pointe, Vermont."

"Where?"

"Holly Pointe." Just saying the name of the town made him smile. "You know, the Capital of Christmas Kindness."

He dropped into an overstuffed chair that sported a moose print.

"I remember taking you kids there." His mother's voice warmed. "It's a lovely town."

"They certainly go all out for Christmas."

"Yes, they do." Puzzlement filled her voice. "But I don't understand why you're there."

Jack kept his tone offhand as he propped his feet on the matching hassock. "I took three people home whose flights were also canceled."

"You did what? Jack, how could you get into a car with strangers?"

"I was going to get onto a plane with strangers. At least in the car, I was in the driver's seat."

"That's not the same, and you know it. Why were you renting a car to begin with? I assumed you would stay in the city."

"Since I planned to be out of town anyway, I thought I'd go to the cabin for a few days. The rental car desk was a madhouse, but I managed to get the last car at that rental car company. I happened to be in the line near other passengers from the same flight and thought I'd help them out. Spirit of the season and all. Two live in Walker. One lives here in Holly Pointe."

"That was kind of you." His mother's voice dropped. "I'm sorry I didn't believe you about your flight being canceled. It's just that I knew you didn't really want to come and—"

"It's okay." Jack cut her off, not wanting to get into wedding talk. "That computer glitch upended a lot of people's holiday plans."

"Are you still planning to go to the cabin?"

"That was the original plan, but I may hang around here for a while. See what the hype is all about."

"I hate that you have to be there alone. Holiday activities are more enjoyable with a friend." His mother paused for just a second, not nearly long enough for him to change the subject.

The last thing Jack wanted was anyone feeling sorry for him.

"Is the guy you dropped off there nice?" The hopeful note in her voice had guilt surging. "Perhaps you and he—"

"Mom," he interrupted. "Seriously, you don't need to worry. The people in this town are friendly. I'll be fine. I plan to immerse myself in local activities."

Jack wasn't sure why he didn't correct his mother and tell her that he'd brought a woman, not a man, to Holly Pointe. Unless it was because, ever since Sam and Natalie got together, she'd been pushing for him to find *someone special*. As if that would make everything okay.

"It sounds like you're going to have a wonderful Christmas even though you won't be with us." His mother's voice thickened with emotion. "That makes me very happy."

"I'll tell you all about my experiences here next time I see you." Jack was considering the best way to end the call when his mother spoke.

"Your brother was disappointed that you wouldn't be here,

but I assured him you tried, told him all about the problems at the airport. He understands."

What did she expect him to say to that? Jack wondered.

"I should let you go." Forget ending the call graciously, he thought. Time to simply end it. "Tell Dad and…everyone to enjoy the weather there."

"I will. I love you, Jack."

"Love ya, too."

Jack clicked off then and set the phone on the small table next to the chair. Idly, he shifted his gaze out the window and saw that it was snowing again.

He smiled.

Having the flight canceled and being unable to rebook until the twenty-ninth had been the answer to a prayer. He didn't mind being in Holly Pointe. In fact, he thought, glancing around the cabin, this might just end up being a good Christmas after all.

After speaking with his mother, Jack did what he did every morning—he reviewed the overnight developments, looking for anything that could impact the firm's investments. As he was technically on vacation, his team would also be reviewing the performance and progress of the firm's current portfolio companies. Still, he preferred to stay informed.

Once that was done, Jack sat back and mentally ran through what he wanted to do with his day. He needed to buy some winter clothing, including a coat, some warm boots and, he thought with a grin, an ugly sweater from Festive Frump. Yesterday, he'd spotted one that seemed perfect, considering the circumstances that had brought him here. It featured a snowman wearing sunglasses, a Hawaiian shirt and flip-flops. The snowman was surrounded by palm trees, seashells and a beach umbrella. Knitted waves and sun motifs added to the design, if you could call it that.

Before any of that, he would begin his day at Rosie's Diner. He told himself he was eager to check it out because the old-school aesthetic reminded him of the places he and his father had enjoyed. While that was true, the real allure was the chance he might run into Melinda.

Melinda was the first woman since Natalie whom he'd found himself interested in on more than a superficial level. There was a depth to Melinda that he'd only begun to explore. And the heat that had flared from the kiss in front of her house had told him he wasn't ready to leave, not Holly Pointe nor her.

He'd considered texting Melinda to let her know that he had decided to stay for a few days, but he had no doubt that her friend Kate had already given her the heads-up.

The short walk to Rosie's went quickly, and when he stepped inside, Jack was greeted with a rush of warm air, the smell of fried food and the happy sound of laughter and conversation.

The two servers, one a middle-aged woman with dark brown hair and a sleeve tattoo and the other a perky blonde teenager, moved efficiently, taking orders and bringing food out from the kitchen. A boy, who also looked to be in his teens, cleared and wiped down tables.

To his calculating eye, business appeared brisk. All but two tables were currently occupied. The older woman, who Jack guessed must be Melinda's mother, greeted him with a warm smile.

"Welcome to Rosie's." She inclined her head. "How many today?"

"One." Jack had learned that in many eateries, eating solo often resulted in speculative glances.

If Rosie thought it strange that he would be eating alone, she didn't show it.

He followed her to a table for two against a far wall, where she pulled out a chair for him. "I hope you're enjoying your stay in Holly Pointe."

"So far, so good." Taking the plastic menu she handed him, Jack glanced around. "This is a nice place."

"Thank you." Rosie smiled. "We have great food and the best coffee in Holly Pointe. That said, can I get you a cup while you check out our menu?"

"Sure. Sounds good." He smiled and studied her more closely, trying to see any trace of Melinda in her.

Rosie's auburn hair was really more brown mixed with gray. Though it held a decided red cast, it couldn't compare to Melinda's rich red tones. Her eye color was brown, not hazel. The only resemblances he could find were in the oval face and the wide mouth.

"I'll be right back." She turned toward the kitchen, but stopped on her way to talk to a group of older men drinking coffee and taking up three smaller tables that had been shoved together.

She returned to Jack's table seconds later with a white ceramic cup that sported a thin green line around the top rim and a full pot of coffee.

Setting the cup on the table, she filled it, leaving room for cream, then smiled. "Bethany will be right over to get your order. Enjoy."

He noticed that on her way back to the area behind the counter, she refilled the older men's cups.

Studying the menu, Jack realized two things—increasing revenue for the diner would be as simple as charging more than a dollar for coffee with unlimited refills and raising other prices that seemed stuck in the twentieth century.

After giving his order to Bethany, the young blonde with a tattoo that said Be Brave in cursive on her inner forearm, Jack sipped his coffee and glanced around. The place had a kitschy kind of charm. He was certainly no expert in restaurant management and décor, but he could see how much could be accomplished even with minimal changes.

His breakfast of eggs, toast and hash browns with a side of bacon filled him up. Nothing fancy, just good old-fashioned diner food.

He thought about his father and all the places just like this they'd visited when he was a kid. Pulling out his phone, he took a picture of the diner and sent it to his father with a quick text.

Checking out a diner. Food gets an A+.

"How was your breakfast?"

Jack looked up, and there was Rosie, doing what a good owner or manager should be doing—making sure guests were happy with the service and with the food.

"Food was great." He gestured to his empty plate. "Bethany kept me well supplied with coffee. I'll definitely be back."

"I'm pleased to hear that."

"You're the owner?" Jack asked before she could step away.

"I am." She held out her hand. "Rose Kelly. Everyone calls me Rosie. I don't believe we've met before."

"Jack McPherson. You're right, we haven't met before." He gave her hand a firm shake and offered her an easy smile. "I'll be in Holly Pointe through the holidays."

"Well, you couldn't have picked a better time to visit." Rosie's lips tipped upward. "This time of year, there's magic in the air."

"Have you lived here long?" The diner had cleared out since he'd arrived, with only him and the group of men remaining.

"All my life."

Jack brought his never-empty coffee cup to his lips. "How long have you owned the café?"

Rosie laughed, and he was reminded of Melinda.

"Feels like my entire life." She expelled a heavy breath. "Owning a café is hard work."

"I've known a few people in the restaurant business." Jack sipped his coffee again. "They said it's a 24/7 job."

"It is, and when you start to receive mailings from Medicare and Social Security, you begin to wonder if this is all there is to life. Or if this is how you want the rest of your life to go." Rosie laughed again. "Then again, this is what I know, and it's what I love." She gestured to the group of men. "These guys are all retirees. I know most of them from high school. They were several years older than me, of course," Rosie added with a wink.

"Obviously," Jack replied with a laugh.

Rosie's face took on a far-off expression, and she looked over at their table. "Many of them are divorced or have lost their spouses. Their kids live far away. I enjoy seeing them every day, talking to them as they enjoy their coffee and conversation. I like knowing I'm making their lives better."

"You're providing a service to the community."

"I guess in a way I am." She paused and studied his face. "What do you do for a living, Mr. McPherson?"

"Please, call me Jack," he told her. "I run a private-equity firm in New York City."

A thoughtful look crossed Rosie's face. "I bet you know a lot of financial types."

"I know my share." He tried to figure out where she was going with this, but came up empty.

"Know anyone interested in buying a café?"

Jack kept his face expressionless. "Are you interested in selling?"

"I'm not sure," she admitted. "But I'm starting to think changes need to be made, and I'm not sure I want to tackle that much work. I'd like to speak with someone knowledgeable who can maybe give me some insight into the best course to take."

"Is there no one in town you can talk to?" Recalling his conversation with Melinda, Jack pressed, "A partner, maybe? Or employees you're mentoring?"

"No, no one local in that line of work and no partner." Rosie's tone remained matter-of-fact. "As far as employees go, there's the cook and a couple waiters, and my daughter, who's been helping me, but no one looking to take over."

"Really?" Jack kept his voice as casual as hers. "Not even your daughter?"

Rosie shook her head. "Melinda has been wonderful. She came home to help me when I needed her, but the diner has never been her dream. It was mine."

Which, Jack realized, matched what Melinda had told him.

"If you don't know anyone…" Rosie began.

"Actually, I do know someone. If you give me your contact information, I'll pass that along to Lara Edwards, a woman I know who specializes in turning around restaurants." Jack paused. "Lara is amazing. She has considerable experience and expertise in the restaurant industry. Best of all, she understands the challenges and opportunities involved in both the renovation and the acquisition process."

"Sounds like just the woman I need to speak with. Be right back." Rosie returned with a weathered business card that included all her contact information. "I'd like to speak with her as soon as possible."

"Are you thinking before the holiday or after?" *As soon as possible* meant different things to different people.

"Before, if possible." Rosie gave a little laugh. "But I know she's probably busy with her own Christmas plans, so after works, too."

Answer received and understood. Jack smiled. "Knowing Lara, you'll likely hear from her sooner rather than later once you get in touch with her. She's always working."

"Like I said, whenever it works." Rosie's eyes now held a hint of sadness. "Sounds as if she's a hardworking young woman. While I admire that quality, I hope she takes time to smell the roses. It's not something I did, and it's definitely something I regret."

Smell the roses? Jack nearly chuckled aloud. He couldn't imagine Lara Edwards taking time to do anything but work.

"Even if she doesn't get back to me, thank you for the referral."

"Oh, she'll get back to you," he said with a brash confidence born of experience. "And I'm happy to help."

"Well, I appreciate it." Rosie studied him for a long moment. "Is there a Mrs. McPherson?"

He laughed. "If you're referring to my mother, yes, there is."

Rosie joined in his laughter.

"It's too bad you're not sticking around longer. My daughter could use a nice young man like you in her life."

CHAPTER TWELVE

Once outside the diner, Jack composed an email to Lara, giving her Rosie's name and telling her that she owned a diner and might be getting in touch. He added that Rosie was a friend and it would mean a lot to him if she would speak with her.

Jack hesitated for a moment before sending the email. To Melinda, Lara could look like a big, bad outsider coming in to exploit Holly Pointe. For a second, he wondered if he'd done the right thing giving Rosie's contact information to Lara.

As he and Lara did business together, he had no doubt Lara would call Rosie. But would Rosie have changed her mind about speaking with someone by then and blow Lara off?

What had Melinda said? That her mom might talk about making changes, but in the end, she would never make a move?

Which meant Rosie probably wouldn't even respond to Lara's efforts to reach her, so no harm done.

With that worry banished, Jack did a little shopping in town, finding the store owners friendly and helpful. He decided to make one final quick stop before heading to Grace Hollow. After placing his purchases in the trunk of his car, he strolled into the Busy Bean.

Standing in line gave him time to study his surroundings as well as the people working efficiently behind the counter.

The interior of the coffee shop, with its rustic wooden furniture and cozy armchairs, practically begged guests to settle in and stay awhile. The soft, warm lighting cast a comforting glow and was obviously designed to make the place feel like a home away from home.

Local artwork and photographs on the walls showcased the town's history and talent of its residents. Across the room, Jack spotted a bulletin board displaying flyers about upcoming community events.

Children hovered near a festively decorated vintage mailbox labeled Santa's Mailbox. After watching several kids place letters inside the mailbox, Jack shifted his gaze to the Christmas tree.

Instead of what he considered normal holiday ornaments, there were folded coffee filters shaped like snowflakes and garlands made of tiny coffee beans. At the top of the tree, a bright star fashioned from red paper coffee cups added a pop of color.

What he found puzzling were the brightly colored tags hanging from the tree that said things like "small coffee," "large hot cocoa" or "muffin."

A loud "ho-ho-ho" had him turning his gaze toward the counter. Jack recognized Kenny immediately. Even if he hadn't been in the shop Melinda had mentioned he owned, no one looked more like Santa Claus than this guy. With his flowing white beard and mustache, rosy cheeks and a laugh that couldn't help but make you smile, he was definitely Santa's doppelgänger.

As the line moved and he inched closer to the counter, Jack focused on the task at hand, studying the selections on the large whiteboard. Though he wasn't big on flavored drinks, it seemed a shame not to try one at this time of year.

Melinda had been right—names mattered. When he stepped forward, he'd narrowed his choice down to two—the Reindeer

Roast, a dark roast coffee, and Santa's Sip, which contained espresso, but he wasn't sure what else.

"Welcome to the Busy Bean, young man." Kenny's voice boomed, and his eyes twinkled. "What can I get you?"

Jack was glad there was still a line of people behind him, or he had the feeling Kenny would know everything about him by the time he walked out the door. "What does the Santa's Sip have in it?"

"For that drink, my gorgeous wife over here," Kenny gestured to a woman with a round face and salt-and-pepper hair busily working the coffee machine, "will top off the espresso and steamed milk with a generous dollop of sweetened whipped cream, then sprinkle it with a pinch of cocoa powder. If you'd like, she can also drizzle some peppermint syrup or chocolate sauce over the top. Do you want my recommendation?"

"Sure."

The old man leaned close as if he were about to impart a secret. "Get it with the peppermint syrup."

Jack grinned. "You've convinced me. I'll take a large."

Kenny beamed. "That's the spirit."

As Jack paid for the drink, he noticed a woman taking one of the tags off the tree before stepping into the line. He gestured with one hand toward the tree. "What's with the tags?"

"Those are Secret Santa gifts." Kenny's eyes took on a warm glow. "Customers have the option to buy Secret Santa items. Those who might not be able to afford a drink or something to eat can take a tag from the tree and get the item on it for free."

"Really?" Jack had heard of Secret Santa gifts, but this was an interesting variation.

"Yep." Kenny handed Jack his change. "At the end of the season, the value of whatever didn't get taken off the tree is donated to the local food bank."

Christmas kindness in action, Jack thought. He opened his wallet, pulled out a hundred-dollar bill and handed it to Kenny.

Surprise flickered in the older man's eyes. "What's this for?"

"I'd like to buy a hundred dollars' worth of free coffee for the tree."

Kenny's gaze shifted from Jack to the tree, then back again. "That's very generous."

"It's Christmas."

"Yes, it is, and I thank you for this." Kenny inclined his head. "If you give me your name, I can include it on the tags."

Jack smiled. "Make the gifts from Santa."

All day, Melinda checked her phone, hoping for a call or text from Jack letting her know that he was still in Holly Pointe. She was curious why he'd stayed and how long he planned to be here.

Despite him paying Kate to rent the cabin for the rest of December, she knew that outlay wouldn't keep him in Holly Pointe if he decided he was ready to leave. He'd likely paid more than he'd given Kate for a single night at a posh hotel.

Which meant he could have simply spent the night and was already in the mountains by now.

Or maybe, and she liked this option best, he'd decided to act on her suggestion to experience all Holly Pointe had to offer at this time of year.

She still hadn't heard from him when the time came for her to sort through her vast array of ugly-sweater options and decide which one to wear tonight. Despite rolling her eyes every Christmas when she opened another package from her brother that contained a sweater, the gesture was only for form. She'd grown fond of the tradition and actually looked forward to seeing what he'd picked out for her.

Tonight, the sweater receiving the nod featured a bold and exaggerated image of a grumpy gingerbread man.

Mr. Grumpy sported crossed arms, a frowning mouth and

mismatched candy buttons. It seemed apropos that surrounding him were scattered gumdrops, frosting drips and candy cane accents.

It brought back memories of how, when their gingerbread house had collapsed, she and Jack had sat in stunned silence for only a second before bursting into laughter. Once they'd regained their composure, they'd munched on gumdrops straight off the roof.

Such a delightful memory.

Now that the sweater had been chosen, Melinda moved on to hair and makeup. She was just pulling on her boots when Kate texted that she was in the driveway.

They were nearly to Grace Hollow when Melinda casually asked Kate if she'd seen Jack today.

"I didn't see him at all, until I saw his car go past my cabin right before I left to pick you up." Kate shot her a sideways glance. "I assumed he was with you today."

"Nope." Melinda did her best to keep the disappointment from her voice, but couldn't quite manage it. "If you hadn't told me he'd rented a cabin, I'd have thought he was in the White Mountains."

"Based on how well you got along on the drive here, and the fact that he stayed, I'm surprised you didn't hear from him."

Melinda shrugged. "Maybe we didn't get along as well as I thought we did."

Then she remembered the laughter, conversation and kisses they'd shared. No, there had been chemistry and interest...and not just on her side.

By the time they reached Grace Hollow, the parking lots were well on their way to being full. It took Kate several minutes to find an open space. Some of the cars likely belonged to last-minute shoppers visiting the Christmas Marketplace, but Melinda bet much of the traffic came from those attending the Ugly Sweater Mixer.

The first friends she and Kate spotted across the room when they stepped into the Baby Barn were Dustin Bellamy and Krista Ankrom. The married couple were surrounded by admirers. Not surprising, as the former NHL star and the supermodel ended up being the center of attraction wherever they went.

Since they'd arrived in Holly Pointe the night before Melinda had left for the airport, she hadn't had a chance to welcome them back to town.

That was definitely on her to-do list for the evening.

Melinda and Kate quickly found themselves in the midst of holiday cheer as they strolled around the barn. They stopped every few steps to greet various friends, then paused to watch a group of five in their early twenties do what she dubbed a Jingle Bell Jump.

While a tall boy with shaggy brown hair videoed, the others sprang into the air, knees raised high, while shaking their hands vigorously.

"What's with the crazy hand gestures?" Kate asked, her brows pulled together in puzzlement.

"I believe they're shaking imaginary jingle bells." Melinda pointed. "See? They're yelling, 'Jingle all the way.'"

"I love their energy." Kate smiled. "It's infectious. I find myself wanting to join in."

"Let's do it."

"Are you serious?"

The question and the excitement in her friend's voice had Melinda getting the okay from the group leader, and then both of them jumped into the hilarity.

By the time the group disbanded, she and Kate were out of breath and laughing.

"It's going to be hard to top that," Kate declared, her face flushed and her eyes sparkling.

"We'll find a way," Melinda promised, unable to stop the grin.

She spotted her brother across the room, wearing the same

Grinch sweater that was his go-to whenever the words *ugly sweater* and *party* were spoken in the same sentence.

Zach, Derek's friend and partner in their construction firm, wore black. The color might seem an odd choice, but it provided the perfect backdrop to the tangle of colorful Christmas lights across his chest that blinked like they were hooked up to a generator on steroids.

Knowing the tight deadline they had on their current project, Melinda was surprised both men had taken time off from work to play. Then she remembered Derek telling her that he wanted to show his daughter the importance of a balanced lifestyle. Which meant working hard during the day and making time for a social life in the evening.

She looked for his girlfriend, Shiloh, but didn't see her. Perhaps she and Camryn were getting a pic taken together at the DIY Ugly Sweater Photo Booth.

As if merely thinking of her beloved niece conjured her up, Melinda heard Camryn say her name right before she found herself enveloped in a mega hug.

"I hoped you'd come." Camryn gave her a hard squeeze before stepping back.

There was so much of Derek in his daughter, Melinda thought. The same blonde hair and, more than that, the same grit and determination that had allowed Derek to take on raising a child as a single father when he'd still been in high school.

"I love your sweater." Melinda smiled at her niece. "Especially the reindeer's googly eyes."

Kate studied Camryn's sweater and nodded. "Super cute."

"Thanks. It's okay. I mean, it doesn't suck." Camryn turned to Melinda. "I heard about your trip blowing up. Now that sucks."

"It does," Melinda agreed. "But I'm planning on scheduling another trip, maybe this spring."

"If you need a travel buddy..." Camryn pointed to herself. "Just remember, I'm available."

"Wait, what about me? I say no one time, and I'm off the travel-buddy list forever?" said Kate, who'd stepped slightly back for the reunion, her tone teasing.

"You'd come with us, Kate," Camryn assured her. "The three of us would have a blast."

Out of the corner of her eye, Melinda noticed Derek still hanging with Zach. "Is Shiloh here?"

Camryn nodded. "She's singing tonight. She'll be taking the stage any minute."

"I love listening to her sing. She has such a fabulous voice." Kate might have said more, but something in the distance appeared to catch her friend's eye. "Eileen's waving me over. I'll catch you two later."

Kate's independent nature was only one of the many things Melinda liked about her. They could attend a function together, but not be joined at the hip.

"You know how to find me." Melinda glanced down at her sweater. "Just look for the grumpy gingerbread man."

"If you stumble across another fun adventure, be sure and track me down." A second later, Kate disappeared into the crowd.

"Adventure?" Interest sparked in Camryn's blue eyes.

Melinda explained about the jingle bell dance.

"You should have found me," Camryn told her, pretending to pout.

"Next time," Melinda promised.

Giving a sudden squeal, Camryn waved wildly, then turned back to Melinda. "I'll catch you later."

As Camryn dashed off toward her friends, Melinda once again let her gaze sweep the room. Shiloh now stood beside her brother. She watched Derek wrap his arms around her.

Shiloh kissed him enthusiastically before climbing the steps to the stage, a satisfied smile on her red lips.

Everything was so easy between them. It had been that way from the beginning. Shiloh wasn't what Melinda would have imagined for Derek, not with her love of performance and desire to be in the spotlight, but she certainly seemed to make him happy.

Same with her mother and Carl. While the retired salesman might not be who Melinda would have picked for her mom, he was a nice guy, and Melinda couldn't recall the last time she'd seen her mom so happy.

Love came so easily to them.

What am I doing wrong here? Melinda wondered as she wandered in Krista's direction.

She had nearly reached her friend when she spotted Jack. He stood in one of the bar lines, chatting with Dustin.

The sweater he wore, with a snowman in a Hawaiian shirt and flip-flops, had her snorting out a laugh. It was the same ugly sweater they'd joked about after seeing it in the Festive Frump booth.

Dustin turned to order, and Jack's gaze shifted. When he spotted her, those amazing lips that had tasted like gumdrops widened into a smile.

Feeling the punch, Melinda couldn't help but smile back, suddenly warm all over.

"Who's the guy with my husband?"

Melinda turned at the sound of Krista's voice and smiled a welcome. The former supermodel looked gorgeous—as always—in a blue sweater featuring a whimsical winter wonderland theme.

"His name is Jack McPherson. He and I were on the same flight to Mexico." Melinda gave a little laugh. "Or, rather, we were supposed to be on that flight."

"That's right. You were going to spend the holiday in Mexico." With a casually elegant gesture, Krista flipped a strand of dark hair over her shoulder. "What happened?"

Melinda quickly explained all that had transpired, ending

with Jack apparently deciding to remain in Holly Pointe for a while longer.

Krista's lips curved. "He stayed because of you."

"I don't know about that. I had to hear from Kate that he'd rented a cabin. My guess is he's here because he wanted to see what Holly Pointe is like at Christmas."

"Yes, and I'm Santa Claus."

"Then can I have a ride to Mexico on your sleigh, Santa?"

Krista laughed. "Okay, okay. A desire to experience a Holly Pointe Christmas may be part of the reason he's here, but trust me, it's not all. You're the real draw."

"Maybe." Melinda had to admit, but only to herself, that the thought gave her a thrill.

Before Melinda could say anything more, the sweet, yet sultry, sounds from the stage of "All I Want for Christmas Is You" filled the barn.

"Shiloh has an incredible voice, such beautiful tone." Krista gestured with her head. "Your brother can't take his eyes off of her."

Derek appeared mesmerized. He stood at the edge of the stage, his gaze firmly fixed on Shiloh, who wore a Santa hat and a red dress the same color as her lipstick.

"Aww, look, Camryn and her friends are there, too." Krista expelled a happy breath. "It's like they're already a family."

Melinda nearly reminded Krista that Derek and Shiloh had been dating for only a few months, but closed her mouth. She had to admit she was amazed at how quickly the two had seemed to connect. The pragmatic part of her said that anything that came that fast couldn't be real. Then she thought of the strong feelings she felt for Jack after less than forty-eight hours.

She wondered if she would ever fall in love. Alex was a great guy, but she hadn't been able to love him.

Once again, her thoughts turned to Jack and the intensity of her attraction. Did having those feelings for a man she'd just met mean she wasn't totally immune to love?

"Will I see you at the pond later?"

Melinda stared blankly at Krista.

"Starlit Skatefest?" Krista reminded her.

"That's right." Another new activity added to the bursting Holly Pointe calendar. "Kate and I talked on the way here about checking it out."

"Dustin and I are going. It'll be fun." Krista gestured with one hand. "Jack should come, too."

Melinda's gaze followed Krista's gesture to where the two men talked as if they were old friends.

It was a skill, that ability to make others like and trust you. She had no doubt that was a necessary skill in Jack's line of work, one he'd honed to perfection.

"I hope things work out for the two of you. It'd be nice for you to have him around to spend time with over the holidays."

Krista was one of the most independent and self-assured women Melinda knew. She'd built a successful career as a model, then segued that popularity into a popular syndicated television show, *Down Home with Dustin & Krista*.

Which was why hearing her suggest that any woman might be happier with a man at her side over the holidays took Melinda by surprise. "I'm perfectly comfortable going to events by myself or with a friend."

Krista's cobalt-blue eyes softened as she laid a hand on Melinda's arm. "I didn't say that very well. I simply thought that this year, with your brother and mother coupled up, it might be fun for you to have someone at your side. Just for Christmas. It would also be nice for Jack, since he doesn't know anyone here."

"He's a social guy. I don't think he'll have any trouble finding women or men to spend time with while he's in Holly Pointe."

"Probably not." Krista spoke in a matter-of-fact tone. "But I've seen him watching you. From those smoldering looks, it's clear to me that it's you he wants to spend time with. Is it that he doesn't interest you?"

"Oh, I'm interested, but what's the point?"

Krista arched an eyebrow. "The point?"

"He'll be here for Christmas, then gone. If he even stays that long."

"All the better if you're not looking for anything permanent." Krista's lips curved. "This could be your resort romance minus the messy sand and hot sun. You can enjoy each other's company without the expectation of more. How often does one get that opportunity?"

Melinda had to admit that when she'd planned her vacation to Mexico, she'd hoped she might meet an unattached guy there. Someone to dance with and maybe share a few kisses with under the stars.

Perhaps if the flights hadn't been delayed, she'd have met Jack at the resort, and they'd have spent time there together.

"You're right." Melinda shook her head and offered a self-deprecating smile. "I'm overthinking again."

"It's easy to worry about being hurt."

"My feelings I can handle," Melinda admitted. "It's always the guy's feelings that concern me."

Melinda could see the puzzlement on Krista's face. Because she felt she needed to explain, but didn't want to blast it to the world, she lowered her voice. "When I lived in Burlington, I dated this guy. I liked him a lot and enjoyed our time together. But when he told me he loved me, I couldn't say it back. He said I broke his heart."

Krista's brows pulled together. "Are you seriously concerned that, over the course of a few days, Jack will fall madly in love with you, and you will break his heart?"

Laughing, Melinda shook her head. "Said that way, it does sound ridiculous."

"Not ridiculous." Krista chuckled. "Just unlikely."

"Um, thanks?"

"I didn't mean it like that. I really am tripping on my words tonight." Krista offered Melinda a smile. "You are lovely and wonderful, and I've no doubt you could break all the hearts you wanted. What I meant was, in real life, people don't fall in love in three days. That's the stuff of novels and movies."

Krista turned her head to look at Jack, still speaking with Dustin but glancing over at Melinda every couple of seconds as if he couldn't focus on anything else. "Then again, anything is possible."

CHAPTER THIRTEEN

It might be silly, but every time Melinda attended a party in her hometown, she felt like Holly Pointe royalty. Of course, she'd never admit that aloud. But having people call out her name, give her hugs and snap pics with her made her feel special.

Melinda had stepped away from an enjoyable conversation with Kenny and Norma when she felt a tap on her shoulder. She whirled.

Seeing Jack standing so close, smiling at her, had her heart skipping a beat.

The blue eyes he settled on her were as warm as his voice when he said her name. "Melinda."

"I thought that was you I saw earlier across the room." She spoke casually, her tone displaying none of the excitement that had her stomach jittering.

Jack grinned. "When I spotted that gingerbread sweater, I said to myself, 'Now there's a woman worth knowing.'"

"You already know me," she responded in a droll tone.

"Oh, Melinda, we've barely scratched the surface."

"You're right. It's crazy to think how close we came to not meeting at all." Melinda thought of the time they'd spent together on the drive back to Holly Pointe. "Even though we were headed to the same destination, unless we'd been seated next to each other on the flight, we never would have met."

"We would have met." He spoke so confidently she was tempted to believe him.

"Kate mentioned you rented a cabin from her. What happened to the White Mountains?"

Jack shrugged. "That was one option. But when a woman I met on vacation recommended I experience Holly Pointe at Christmas, I decided to take her advice."

"Hmmm, she sounds very wise and beautiful."

"Eh, she's okay."

Melinda smacked his arm with the back of her hand.

He laughed.

"Actually, you're right. She is very smart, and very funny, very kind, very, very beautiful, and," Jack brought his lips close to her ear and lowered his voice, "a very good kisser."

Heat rose up her neck, and Melinda had to fight to regain her composure. She cleared her throat. "I have a question for you."

"Shoot."

She kept her tone casual. "I was surprised you didn't text to let me know you decided to stay."

"Well…" He paused to tuck a stray strand of hair behind her ear with a finger. "Based on the chain of communication during the car ride, I figured Kate would tell you."

"Hearing it from her wasn't the same as hearing it from you."

"I should have texted. Or called. I love hearing your voice." His lips quirked upward, then his expression sobered. "The truth is, I got busy with work and then did some shopping."

"Shopping?"

"Winter clothes and," he pointed to his chest, "this amazing sweater."

Melinda chuckled. "It suits you."

"I'm not sure that's a compliment."

This time, she laughed.

"Not to change the subject, but Dustin mentioned there's another event going on this evening."

"Starlit Skatefest at Spring Lake. It's new this year." Melinda thought of how long it had been since she'd skated under a star-filled sky. "It should be a blast."

"Does that mean you're going?"

"I thought I might."

"What a coincidence." He offered a heart-stopping smile. "I'm thinking I might, too."

Her heart gave two solid thumps against her chest before she reminded herself that he hadn't brought up them going together. Then again, neither had she.

Play it safe, Melinda told herself, then thought, *to heck with that.* "Kate and I talked about going together. Why don't you come with us?"

～

Moments later, they turned toward the sound of raucous laughter.

"I mentioned my mom's boyfriend, Carl." Melinda gestured with one hand. "That's him."

Carl was entertaining a group of men and women by making reindeer antlers, candy cane wands and Santa Claus hats out of balloons.

When Eileen put a balloon Santa hat on her head, the group clapped and cheered.

Rosie slipped to Carl's side, and the older man looped an arm around her shoulders.

"I'm taking orders," he said in a booming voice. "Who's next?"

Jack gestured with his head as people shouted out requests. "Popular guy."

"Everyone loves Carl, including, it appears, my mom." Melinda's lips tipped in a rueful smile. She started to say more, then changed her mind. "If we're going to get any skating in, we should head to the lake."

"I'm ready to go."

"Let me find Kate."

"Did I hear my name?" Kate smiled at Melinda before shifting her gaze to Jack. "I saw you across the room, but haven't had a chance to say hello. I'm glad I caught you before you left."

"Jack isn't leaving. Well, he is, but he's leaving to go to Skate-fest with us. Not exactly with us," she clarified. "He's going to meet us there."

"Is that right?" Kate's smile remained firmly in place.

"If you don't mind," Jack began. "I—"

"Actually, that works out great." Kate spoke quickly before he had a chance to say more.

Melinda turned back to Jack. "See? I told you she wouldn't mind."

Smiling at Kate, Melinda clarified, "When I mentioned that we had plans, Jack didn't want to intrude. You know, be the third wheel. But I assured him it wouldn't be a problem."

"I'm glad you invited him." Kate brought two fingers to the bridge of her nose and pressed. "I've had a headache most of the day, and it's gotten worse. I was about to tell you that skating was a no-go for me tonight."

"Oh, Kate." Melinda placed a hand on her friend's arm. "You should have said something. We could have left as soon as you started feeling badly."

Melinda remembered them jumping and jingling early in the evening, which meant the headache must not have been bad at the beginning. She forgave herself for not noticing her friend was in pain.

"I was having fun. We both were." Kate's tone held reassurance.

"We'll leave now." Melinda cast Jack an apologetic glance. "You should still go to the Skatefest."

"Melinda, have fun with Jack," Kate rushed on. "I'm going home and straight to bed."

"I could make you some tea or—"

"I'm going straight to bed when I get home," Kate repeated. "If you go with Jack, I won't feel so bad about ruining your evening."

"You didn't ruin my evening." Melinda's gaze searched her friend's face. "How about you let me at least drive you home? Jack can pick me up at your house."

She slanted a glance at Jack and got a nod before refocusing on Kate. "That way, you can just close your eyes and relax instead of concentrating on driving."

"You're so sweet, and I appreciate the offer." Kate gave Melinda's arm a squeeze. "But I'm good enough to drive." Kate turned to Jack. "You'll see she gets home safely?"

"Count on it," Jack told her.

Once Kate had left, Melinda shoved aside her worry by reminding herself Kate was a sensible woman. She'd said she was up to driving home, so she was.

Reaching into her pocket, Melinda pulled out a ticket stub and held it up. "We might as well grab our coats and head to the lake."

Taking her stub, Jack added his to it.

When they reached the coat check counter, Melinda was surprised to see a familiar face. "Bethany. I didn't expect to see you here tonight."

"I work a couple of different jobs." Shifting from one foot to the other, Bethany offered Jack a quick smile. "Including the breakfast shift at the diner."

Melinda smiled. "The customers love her."

"Most of them, anyway," Bethany muttered under her breath, then gestured with one hand. "I don't mean to rush you, but do you have your coat checks? There's a line behind you."

Jack handed her the stubs, along with a fifty.

Bethany gazed at the folded bill in confusion. "There's no charge to check coats."

Melinda had no doubt the girl had been accepting tips all evening, but probably not fifty dollars for two coats.

"Consider it an early Christmas present," Jack told her, then turned to help Melinda on with her coat.

"Are you always such a big tipper?" Melinda asked when they were out of earshot.

"It's Christmas." He smiled. "Can you think of a better time to spread holiday cheer?"

～

Once they were in the car, Jack turned to Melinda. "What's Bethany's deal?"

"What do you mean?"

"Her comment about 'most of the customers.'" Concern filled his blue depths. "Has there been trouble?"

Melinda blew out a breath. "It's not a secret. While it's true most have been supportive, my mom mentioned some of the customers have made remarks about how disappointed they are in her."

Confusion furrowed Jack's brow.

"Sorry, I need to back up." Melinda's tone held no judgment. "Bethany is Pastor Shuck's youngest. She got involved in drugs and ran off last year with some older guy. She was only sixteen. They were eventually found in California. She's back home now, and the family is in counseling."

Sympathy blanketed Jack's face. "Instead of being supported, she's being judged."

"By some," Melinda admitted. "Holly Pointe isn't perfect—nowhere is—but on the whole, we're a kind community."

On the drive to the lake, the discussion about Bethany was as heavy as it got. The ride could have lasted for hours, at least as far as Melinda was concerned. The car was warm, and in the close confines, she basked in the intoxicating scent of Jack's cologne.

She hadn't noticed it earlier—the citrusy scent was oh-so-subtle—but once they were together in the small space, her nose had picked up the scent. For some reason, it made Melinda think about how lovely it had been when they kissed.

"...the diner."

Melinda realized he'd either asked her a question or perhaps made a simple comment. Of course, she didn't have a clue. She'd been too busy thinking about kissing him.

Smiling brightly, she shifted in her seat to face him. "The diner?"

When his lips curved and his gaze dropped to her mouth, she wondered if he'd been having the same kinds of thoughts.

She hoped so.

"I was just saying I had breakfast at Rosie's Diner this morning." He slowed, then turned the car in the direction of the lake without any hesitation, obviously not needing her assistance in finding the way. "I hoped you'd be there."

"I wasn't working today. Now I wish I had been." Melinda was a little surprised this was the first she was hearing of his visit. "What did you think?"

"I thought it was charming." He smiled. "The food was great. Bethany waited on me."

Melinda couldn't hide her surprise. "You didn't say anything."

"She seemed eager to move us along."

Melinda nodded. "Was my mom there?"

"She was." Jack slanted a sideways glance in her direction. "She came by after I finished eating, wanting to know if everything had been satisfactory."

Melinda nodded. "Visiting with customers is what she likes most about owning a diner."

"She's very passionate about the café. She mentioned knowing that changes need to be made, but said she wasn't sure what those should be."

"Here we go again." Melinda waved an airy hand. "Same song, different verse."

"Pardon?"

"I can't tell you how many times she's said that same exact thing to me or to my brother. Like I told you before, she might say she wants to make changes, but when offered possibilities, she backs off." Melinda shrugged. "Her business. Her decisions. I'm out of it."

He cocked his head. "Do you want to be out of it? Truly?"

"I want her to do what she wants. It's good I feel that way," Melinda had to chuckle, "because that's exactly what she's going to do."

All talk of her mother and the diner ended when they pulled into the parking lot adjacent to Spring Lake.

The night was dark, which only made the luminarias and candles lining the pathways around the lake even more impressive.

As she strode down the pathway, Melinda thought how the flickering lights added a romantic and magical ambience to the event. When Jack took her gloved hand in his, she sighed with pleasure.

Twinkling fairy lights, festive garlands and Christmas ornaments that glowed from within seemed even more special when combined with a local choir performing classic Christmas carols and holiday tunes.

This was the first year for the fire pits. They'd been strategically placed around the pond, offering a place where people could gather and roast marshmallows to make s'mores.

"Wow." Instead of heading toward the wooden structure offering skate rentals, Jack paused, taking it all in.

"Goes a little beyond simply skating on a wintry night."

"You've got that right." Jack turned to her, his hand curved loosely around hers. "This is amazing."

"We do it up right in Holly Pointe."

"I'm glad you encouraged me to stay and experience this." He gestured with his free hand.

"I'm glad you decided to stay."

"So am I."

When he leaned over and kissed her gently, the nearly perfect night just got a whole lot brighter.

CHAPTER FOURTEEN

It didn't take Jack long to discover that Melinda's skating skills matched his own. If she'd been a novice, he would have been happy to hold her up as they circled the lake that everyone referred to as a pond.

On the lake, skaters of every age and skill level coexisted peacefully. In the middle, teens practiced their turns, while the majority, including him and Melinda, were content to skate round and round under the fairy lights while the dulcet tones of carols filled the air.

Since they were comfortable on the ice, after skating arm in arm for a while, they took turns skating backward, trusting the other to steer them away from any obstacle.

As she let go of his arm to wave to another person she knew, he smiled. "You seem to really love it here."

She turned back to him and flashed a megawatt smile. "What's not to love?"

He nodded his agreement. "Is this your forever kind of place?"

Instead of tossing off some quick answer, Melinda took a moment before responding. "Well, forever's a long time. I don't know what'll happen forever, but I love it here for so many reasons. And I'm loving showing you my town and spending this time with you."

Melinda's eyes filled with something that looked an awful lot like desire. Or, Jack thought, perhaps that was only his own need he saw reflected in those hazel depths.

As they made another rotation, Jack realized she'd mentioned wanting a s'more when they'd first started skating. At that time, families with little kids had been crowded around the fire pits.

As the night had gone on, most of the young families had left. Now there was room—room for he and Melinda to make more memories.

"Ready for a sweet treat?" he asked, keeping his gaze firmly fixed on her face.

Interest flared in her hazel depths. "What do you have in mind?"

Was it only his imagination, or had her voice taken on a sultry edge?

"I thought we'd have a s'more."

"And afterward," Melinda smiled, "you can drive me home."

Jack made short work of the drive to her house.

Melinda knew the warmth filling the car had little to do with the heat pouring from the vents.

He started to pull the car into the driveway, but seeing the amount of snow that had fallen since she'd left, chose to park out front instead. "That will need to be shoveled. I'll do it for you."

"No worries. I'll do it in the morning." She heaved an exaggerated sigh. "You realize if we were in Mexico right now, the heaviest thing I'd be lifting would be a margarita glass."

"And I'd be at a wedding." His voice turned husky. "Rather than with you now."

She nodded, wondering how she could tell him that she was

starting to believe they'd have found each other, if not during this Christmas season, then at some other time.

Even in her own head, that sounded schmaltzy and sentimental, so she simply reached for the door handle. "Walk me to the door?"

"Of course."

Though she had only recently met him, she wanted him. Wanted to feel his hands and mouth on her bare skin, wanted to wrap her legs around him and draw him close until there was no distance between them.

She had no doubts that Jack would be a kind and considerate lover.

When she got out of the car, he was there, his hand on her arm as if he sensed she was unsteady and wanted to be there to catch her if she fell.

The walkway to her front steps was dry. Even if they had been icy or snow-packed, Melinda possessed a terrific sense of balance. The unsteadiness was less about secure footing and more about how Jack made her feel…all there and gone.

By the time they reached the front door, she'd made her decision. "Come inside for a few?"

He smiled. "I'd like that."

Melinda tended to keep her house tidy, for which she was now thankful. Though it appeared that, as far as Jack was concerned, there could have been clothing everywhere.

Jack didn't seem at all interested in scrutinizing the modest living quarters. Instead, his blue eyes remained firmly focused on her.

When he held out his hands, she hesitated for a moment.

He smiled. "Your coat?"

Feeling foolish, she started to shrug it off. "Good idea."

"Allow me." As he slipped the coat from her shoulders, his knuckles brushed her neck, leaving fire in their wake.

After hanging his coat—and hers—on the coat tree near the

entrance, he pulled her close. Enfolding her into his arms, he kissed her long and slow and sweet.

Melinda wrapped her arms around his neck and threaded her fingers through his soft hair. "Will you stay the night?"

"There is nothing I'd like better." He brushed his lips across hers. A second later, regret skittered across his face. "I don't have protection."

"Then it's lucky for both of us that I have condoms." She kissed him softly. "And I'm on the pill."

"This is my lucky day." His arms slid around my waist. "Or should I say my night?"

"I could be a big dud." Melinda hesitated. "It's been a while."

His hands stroked up and down her back. "There's no way you're a dud."

"How can you be certain?"

"Good point." His blue eyes gleamed with mischief. "We'll know for sure soon enough."

"My bedroom is—"

"Sit for a minute." Taking her hand, he tugged her to the sofa.

Melinda tried to conceal her disappointment. Obviously, he wasn't as hot to get this party started as she was.

He sat beside her on the sofa, then slid his arms around her and began to kiss her. The soft, sweet kisses had her insides turning all gooey. A yearning rose from deep inside her.

Sliding her fingers into his hair, Melinda poured that yearning into her kiss.

The long kiss that followed had her heart pounding. Heat pooled low in her belly, and she ached for his touch.

Still, they kissed. And when his tongue swept across her lips and then plunged deep when she opened her mouth, the heat turned to raw need. It was almost as if he were already inside her.

The kiss ended, and he pushed to his feet.

With her heart pounding in her ears, Melinda could only stare. Was he leaving?

Thank goodness she didn't voice the crazy thought, because he reached down and tugged her to her feet. "Let's check out the bedroom."

By the time they reached the small room with its blue-gray walls and white duvet, need had replaced her nerves.

"Are you sure this is what you want?" he asked, even as he scattered kisses up her neck.

"It is." She smiled. "How else am I to know if I'm a dud?"

He shook his head, the look in his eyes telling her he had not a single doubt. "For all you know, I could be one, too."

"I have a thought." She planted a kiss against his throat, reveling in the salty taste of his skin. "How 'bout we declare this a dud-free zone?"

Sliding his hands up under her sweater, he grinned. "I have another suggestion."

She arched a brow.

"How about we quit talking?"

Melinda was still curled up against Jack's warm body the next morning when her phone rang. Recognizing her mother's ringtone, she glanced at the clock. Not even six a.m.

Melinda knew it had to be some sort of emergency for her mother to call at this hour.

Rolling over, she snatched the phone off the bedside charging stand. "Mom. What's up?"

"Oh, Melinda, I'm so glad you answered." Her mother's voice had that frazzled sound. "A server and one of the busboys called in sick today."

It was the Saturday before Christmas, and Melinda had no doubt that the diner would be swamped all morning.

"I've got enough staff on for lunch, but I really need someone until eleven. I know you're technically on vacation, but could you please come help me?"

"Of course." Melinda thought quickly. The diner opened at six, but the real rush wouldn't start until seven. "I'll be right in."

"Thank you, thank you, thank you. I'm so sorry for calling so early."

"We're family. I want you to call when you need help. You know I'm always here for you." Melinda hated that her mother had for one second hesitated to contact her. "See you soon."

"What's up?"

Jack pushed up on his elbows and shot her a questioning look. He looked so enticing with his hair tousled and a sexy stubble darkening his cheeks.

"My mom had a couple employees call in sick this morning." Melinda couldn't resist. She leaned over and kissed him, but pulled back when his arms slid around her. "I can't stay. She needs help with the morning rush. I should be done by eleven."

Last night, before they'd fallen asleep, they'd made plans to attend the snowman-building contest today. "If you're still interested, I should be done in time to do the snowman thing. If you pick me up at the diner at eleven, we could head straight there."

"I have a better idea." Those brilliant-blue eyes remained fixed on her face. "I'll go with you to the diner, do what I can to help, and we'll leave from there together."

Jack couldn't recall ever busing a table, but he'd cleared more than his share of dishes over the years. He didn't mind helping out Rosie. From the moment he and Melinda walked through the door, it was apparent Rosie hadn't been exaggerating about needing help.

Melinda jumped immediately into taking orders, and he did his best to keep the tables cleared.

Though there were other servers and one other busboy who looked as if he was no more than fourteen, Jack felt as if he and Melinda were a team.

He liked seeing the customers' happy faces—not a Grinch in sight—and there was lots of appreciation expressed for the service and the food.

Though he couldn't take credit for either, he knew that clearing the tables quickly made it possible for those waiting in line to get their morning breakfast more quickly.

Rosie managed the waiting list and the cash register with an ease born of long practice.

Jack noticed she still made it a point to warmly greet unfamiliar guests.

Melinda was the perfect ambassador, not only for the diner, but for Holly Pointe. As he cleared a nearby table, he heard her telling a couple and their two kids about the snowman-building contest.

At another table, she listened respectfully to a couple who had all sorts of menu suggestions, ranging from more vegan options to specialty coffee.

Melinda smiled. "I'll be sure and pass along your thoughts to the owner."

When he and Melinda walked out of the diner shortly after eleven, Jack felt good knowing he'd done his part to help with the morning rush.

"How was it for you?" Melinda asked as they started walking toward the field leading into town.

"Good. I enjoyed myself."

Melinda cast him a skeptical glance.

"Seriously. I like being part of a team. That's what it felt like with all of us working together."

"I love that feeling, too." Melinda's lips curved upward. "I know she didn't have much time to talk, but my mother raved about you. She thinks you're the greatest guy ever. And she isn't the only one who thinks that."

"I've got them snowed."

"They see you for who you are."

Jack didn't want any accolades, certainly didn't deserve them for simply helping out a friend. "Spending time in the café showed me that Rosie's Diner is a special place."

He thought of Lara and hoped that, if she and Rosie did connect, whatever comments or suggestions Lara offered wouldn't take away from that specialness.

"I agree. I love it." Melinda took his hand as they walked. "The diner has been a part of my life since I was a kid."

That sentiment told Jack that Melinda was more emotionally involved with the diner than she had let on.

"There are so many changes that could be made," Melinda continued. "Nothing major, just little changes to the building and to the menu that would make the diner even more special."

The comment made it sound like she was thinking of a future when she would be in charge—totally at odds with the way she'd spoken of the diner before.

"So, that *is* what you want?" he asked. "To take over Rosie's for yourself?"

"I'd never want to displace my mother. The diner will always be hers, not mine." Melinda's expression turned thoughtful. "What I want is for her to be successful so she's not run out of business by a bunch of new restaurants that don't share her history with the town and that are just here to capitalize on the tourists, not be a true part of the community."

"Like Jingle Shells or Sugarplum's?"

"Exactly."

Once again, Jack's thoughts turned to Lara. Melinda would likely view Lara as a big, bad outsider coming in to exploit Holly Pointe. Perhaps he should at least tell her that he'd given her mom Lara's card.

He opened his mouth, but before he could speak, Melinda waved a dismissive hand.

"I've given her so many ideas of how she could bring the diner into the twenty-first century without breaking her budget. She may talk about making changes, but in the end, she always sticks with the status quo."

"That's too bad."

Melinda lifted one shoulder and let it drop. "It is what it is."

Which meant Rosie likely wouldn't respond to Lara's overtures. Which meant no harm, no foul on his part.

Jack squeezed Melinda's hand as laughter and conversation wafted on the breeze. "Sounds like we're nearly there. Bring me up to speed on this snowman-building event."

CHAPTER FIFTEEN

The crispness in the air had everyone at the snowman competition dressed in layers and wearing waterproof gloves. The sunshine and the promise of a fun event had them all in high spirits.

Rosie had slipped away from the diner shortly before Melinda and Jack had walked out the door. As the event coordinator, Rosie needed to take a few hours away from her work at the diner to oversee the competition.

It didn't surprise Melinda to see Carl there. Like Mary and her little lamb, anywhere that Rosie went, Carl was sure to follow.

Sauntering up to the two, Melinda offered both a smile. "I heard the category question finally got decided."

Though there had been much discussion on the issue this fall, since Melinda had planned to be gone during the competition, she hadn't voiced an opinion on how many categories there should be. "How many did you end up with?"

"Three." Rosie glanced down at the sheet of paper attached to a clipboard. "We have Snow People, Snow Animals and Snow

Sculpture. Plus, we created an extra award, Best in Snow. That's my personal favorite," Rosie added with a wink.

Beside her, Jack chuckled.

"Three seems like a good number." Melinda gave an approving nod. "I assume you have criteria for each category?"

Melinda didn't really care about the criteria. She was stalling, which made no sense, because any minute, contestants would be arriving.

"Right here in front of me." Rosie once again glanced down at her clipboard. "Creativity, craftsmanship, use of accessories and overall aesthetic appeal."

"All the flyers and online information encouraged participants to bring their own materials and accessories to decorate the snowmen." Carl jumped into the conversation. "The planning committee thought it'd be a good idea to have some basic supplies available onsite. That's what I'm here for." Carl gestured to several bins located behind the judging table. "For those who may need them, I have scarves, hats, buttons, carrots for noses and broomsticks for arms."

"Sounds like you're prepared." Melinda glanced around. "Where's Gen?"

The last Melinda knew, Genevieve Scott, the art teacher at the high school, was on tap as the other judge.

"She isn't here." Rosie cast a worried glance in Carl's direction. "Perhaps we should try calling her this time instead of texting again."

"I'll do that now." Carl smiled at Melinda and Jack, then pulled out his phone. "Excuse me."

"And the fun begins." Rosie gestured to a large group composed of children and adults approaching them.

She pulled a whistle from her pocket, then blew, the shrill sound piercing the air.

A dozen high school students wearing Santa hats and holding clipboards immediately headed in her direction.

When the teens reached her, Rosie raised her voice to be heard. "As we discussed previously, after checking the participant's registration status, please escort or direct them to the designated area noted next to their name. If they are wanting to register today, send them over to the judging desk, and we'll get them signed up. Make sure to remind everyone of the rules and time limits. Thank you."

With a buzz of excitement rippling in the air, the teens sprang into action.

Carl reappeared, sporting a relieved smile.

"Gen is on her way," he informed Rosie. "She had car trouble, but it's working now. She told me she's five minutes away."

The line of same-day registrants continued to grow.

Melinda gestured to the line. "Looks like you could use some extra hands."

Jack stepped forward. "Tell us how we can help."

~

"They certainly got a good turnout." Jack's gaze scanned the field filled with creative snowmen designs.

A gray-haired reporter from *The Barre-Montpelier Times Argus*, who'd arrived shortly after the competition began, gave an approving nod. "This is more people than I anticipated."

Standing beside Jack, Melinda smiled. "Alice, you should know not to underestimate Holly Pointe."

"I always say I won't make that mistake again. Then I do." Shifting back into work mode, Alice turned to the photographer she'd brought along. "I want lots of pictures of Dustin and Krista. Also, do your best to get some of the boys, though they tend to be protective of the twins."

Without another word to Jack and Melinda, Alice strode to where Dustin and his family had constructed a snowman with a superhero twist. They'd crafted a cape out of a bedsheet, and small branches created superhero arms and hands.

"It's clever how they used nontoxic paint to give the snowman a heroic costume," Melinda said to Jack.

Jack nodded. "Using rocks to create a superhero emblem on its chest is pretty inspired."

She slanted him a sideways glance. "I know we talked about entering the contest. I'm sorry it didn't work out."

"Don't be sorry. I enjoyed helping." Before she realized what was happening, he'd leaned over and brushed her lips with his. "I'll be your wingman anytime."

The feel of his mouth against hers had memories of last night's lovemaking surging.

"Melinda," Shiloh rushed over, "come see our snowman family."

Our, Melinda knew, included her brother and niece.

"You come, too, Jack," Shiloh urged. "It's super awesome."

As they walked up, Derek was putting stones around the dog's neck to look like a collar, while Camryn fine-tuned the cat's eyes. In addition to the two pets, there was a mother, a father and a child.

"Wow." Melinda stared. "They're all decorated differently."

"To reflect their personalities." Camryn shot a glance at Shiloh. "That's Shiloh's brilliance."

"Well, you've certainly gone beyond the traditional three stacked snowballs." Admiration sounded in Jack's voice.

"We entered the Snowpeople category." Camryn brought her gloved hands together. "I hope we win."

"I hope you do, too. Even if you don't, this is a work of art." Melinda met her niece's gaze. "You should be proud."

In the end, Dustin and Krista's snowman superhero didn't win, and neither did her brother and Shiloh's snowman family. Instead, a group from Massachusetts vacationing in the area won Best in Snow for their snowball rock band.

Melinda had to admit the trio of snowmen positioned as a rock band, complete with miniature instruments made from snow and sticks, was impressive. One snowman was obviously the lead singer with a carrot for a microphone. Another played a snow guitar, while the third was on drums, using snowball drumsticks.

After a round of applause for all the entries, Rosie encouraged everyone to take plenty of pictures and post generously on social media. Then, obviously following the script given to her by Stella, Holly Pointe's PR person, Rosie advised all the entrants would receive coupons good for a free cup of hot cocoa at any of the town's freestanding coffee carts.

"Smart move giving the coupons." Shiloh gave an approving nod. "It gets everyone to the shops and makes even those who lost feel like winners."

"We may not have won, but our entry is dope." Camryn's gaze lingered on the snow family.

"And we had a blast." Derek slung one arm around Camryn's shoulders, then the other around Shiloh.

"Do you have time to get a hot cocoa with me and Dad?" Camryn asked Shiloh.

The brunette glanced at her watch. "I've got a little time."

"Shiloh is one of the people overseeing tonight's Christmas Caroling Parade." Pride filled Derek's voice.

"Christmas Caroling Parade?" Puzzlement furrowed Jack's brow.

"It's really cool and just like it sounds," Melinda explained. "A select group of participants walk through the town's streets singing classic Christmas carols and encouraging onlookers to join them."

"Everyone is welcome to walk in the parade, or stand on the sidewalk, if that's what they prefer," Shiloh added. "We hope everyone will at least sing with us."

Melinda turned to Jack. "The Christmas Caroling Parade is

totally unique to Holly Pointe, and something everyone should experience."

Jack grinned. "You don't have to sell me. I'm all in."

$\sim$

A light snow fell as Melinda strolled beside Jack. The street had been closed to traffic, not only to accommodate those taking part in the Christmas Caroling Parade, but for the horse-drawn sleigh rides being offered.

Santa was there, looking regal as he listened to last-minute wishes on the throne set up in front of the Bromley mansion. The once-elegant private home was now a popular venue for parties and events.

Melinda's voice harmonized with Jack's and dozens more as they slowly made their way down the street. Coffee carts, selling everything from seasonal flavored coffee to hot chocolate and mulled cider, were on every corner.

The scent of freshly roasted nuts mingled with the enticing aroma of gingerbread from another stand just a few feet away.

In front of the antique store, light-up toys and glow sticks were arranged in an attractive display to mimic a mini light show. From the line that stretched down the sidewalk, the place was doing a brisk business.

Brightly colored lights encircling the windows of each business provided the perfect contrast to the winter wonderland of snow-packed streets and falling flakes of white.

Melinda tightened her hold around Jack's arm as the last words of the carol "God Rest Ye Merry Gentleman" flowed from her lips. After breathing in the crisp evening air, she heaved a sigh of contentment. "This is so much fun."

He glanced over, and their eyes met. "You look happy."

"I can say unequivocally that, at this moment, there is nowhere I'd rather be than right here." Tossing her head made the jingle bell she'd attached to the tip of her stocking hat fill the air with a joyous sound.

"That bell is going to make you crazy by the end of the evening," he warned.

"It may make *you* crazy, but I get a kick out of hearing it jingle every time I move."

"Love the bell on the hat," a woman called as she passed by.

"Thank you," Melinda called back, then turned to smirk at Jack.

Jack cocked his head. "Friend of yours?"

"Nope, never seen her before." Melinda couldn't resist shaking her head again and making the bell jingle. "Just another person who finds this particular accessory delightful."

Jack laughed. "You're a goof."

Melinda smiled. "Not the first time I've been told that."

When the group launched into "Jingle Bells" as the next selection and Jack reached up to make her hat jingle, Melinda could only laugh.

They'd made it through six of the ten carols when Jack pointed to a horse-drawn sleigh that had just pulled up and was letting out a mother and her two kids. "Take a ride with me."

Melinda glanced from the sleigh to Jack. When she spoke, her voice quivered with excitement. "Are you serious?"

He took her hand. "It's a perfect night for a sleigh ride with you."

Though she'd have had no trouble hopping in under her own power, Melinda let Jack help her into the sleigh. When he settled the provided blanket across their laps, then slipped an arm around her shoulders, Melinda sighed with pleasure.

"How far does this ride take us?" Jack asked the driver, who Melinda recognized as Camryn's band instructor.

"A half a mile one way and then back."

"If I give you a hundred dollars, will you go a couple of miles before you turn back?"

"Jack…" Melinda began.

"You said all the money goes to the cancer center," Jack reminded her. "They've got three sleighs going, and there wasn't a line when this one pulled up."

He was right, Melinda thought, there hadn't been a line. Not only that, when they'd gotten into this one, there had been another sleigh waiting for customers.

"Sure." The driver grinned and added, "And I'll take it real slow."

"Much appreciated." Jack handed him two fifties, then a twenty. "That's your tip. Merry Christmas."

The man grinned, and when he flicked the reins, the sleigh lurched forward.

Jack brushed a kiss against her hair.

"Thanks for doing this for me," she murmured, snuggling against him.

"You're welcome." Jack expelled a contented breath. "I can't recall the last time I felt so relaxed."

Melinda looked up at him. "I'm glad you're here so we can experience all this together."

"Doesn't just a little bit of you wish you were in Mexico instead?"

Her lips curved as she turned her body toward him and lifted her face for his kiss. "Not one little bit."

After the parade, Melinda and Jack joined friends at Holly Jolly's. They sat at the far end of several tables that had been pushed together.

The popular local bar was hopping. Luckily, they'd beaten the rush.

Melinda had meant what she'd told Jack. There was no place she'd rather be than here with him. Mexico was lovely, and she would make it there one day, but today had reminded her that Holly Pointe was the best place to spend the holidays.

Holly Jolly's might not offer sun and sand, but they had delicious margaritas.

A perky college girl was their server this evening. "What can I get you to drink?"

Melinda thought for a second. "White Christmas Margarita."

Across the table, Lucy's blue eyes sparkled. "Make that two."

"Add a couple more plates of loaded nachos to my tab," Trevor called.

Melinda offered Lucy's husband an indulgent smile and gestured to the plate of nachos that sat at the other end of the table. "How many plates of nachos can you eat, Trev?"

"Those are for you and Kate." He grinned, then shrugged. "If you want to share. That's your decision."

"Mel will share with me." Derek pulled out a chair. "Right, sis?"

"I suppose." Melinda shot a conspiratorial glance at Jack, who was just returning to the table after stepping away to take a call. "A little warning, Jack. You may need to fight to get your share of the nachos. My brother loves 'em."

Jack gave an absent smile.

"Is everything okay?" Melinda whispered when he dropped down into the chair that he'd vacated minutes earlier.

"My mother called to tell me about the wedding. Apparently, Sam and Natalie were married this morning just as the sun was coming up. Mom said it was lovely, but I was missed."

Melinda gave his arm a comforting squeeze.

"I spoke briefly with my brother and with Natalie and wished them a long and happy life together." His shoulders relaxed as if a weight had slipped from them.

Jack shifted his attention to the stage, as if ready to change the subject. "I didn't realize Shiloh was performing."

"She's everywhere lately." Melinda had been predisposed to

like anyone her brother liked, and she genuinely liked Shiloh. Most of all, she wanted Derek to be happy. Goodness knew the course of his love life had been rockier than Melinda's.

Until Shiloh, his past relationships had been short-lived. For the past fourteen years, his primary focus had been on raising his daughter.

"What's Camryn up to tonight?" Melinda asked.

"Spending the night with Lissa." Derek sipped his beer. "They're having their own Christmas party, exchanging gifts, that kind of thing."

Melinda remembered her own happy teenage years. "Sounds like fun."

The extra plates of nachos arrived, and everyone around the table dove in, including Melinda.

Kate picked up a nacho loaded with meat, cheese, guac and jalapeños. "Thanks for ordering these."

"Thank Trevor, not me," Derek said.

Kate shot a smile at Trevor and gave him the thumbs-up.

"I was starving." Kate's hair, cut short in a flouncy collarbone cut, set off her heart-shaped face. Her glasses, tortoiseshell cat-eyed frames, fit her studious, thoughtful nature to perfection.

Melinda had always thought Kate and Derek would be good together, but though they'd built a solid friendship over the years, whatever there was between them had never evolved into more.

"How was your day?" Melinda asked when her friend finished off her second nacho, then wiped her fingers clean on a paper napkin. "Headache all gone, I hope."

For a second, Kate looked blank, then shook her head.

"I'm good." Kate reached for another nacho. "I love their nachos."

"I love their margaritas." Prettily topped with a lime wedge and fresh cranberries, the concoction made Melinda smile as she brought the glass to her lips.

Casting a sideways glance, Melinda found Jack's attention focused on the stage while he visited with her brother.

She studied his handsome profile, and her heart skipped a beat. The cologne he wore tonight was subtle, but since the chairs were shoved so close, the scent teased her nostrils.

While listening to Shiloh sing Christmas ballads, Jack and her brother discussed what teams they expected to see in the Super Bowl. Melinda discovered Jack's knowledge of the sport matched her brother's.

It was crazy to think that last week she hadn't known him, and now she was having difficulty imagining her life without him in it. She remembered when she'd told Krista she was worried he would fall in love with her and she'd break his heart.

She sure had gotten that wrong.

It wasn't his heart at risk—it was hers.

CHAPTER SIXTEEN

The Christmas Eve candlelight service the next day at the Holly Pointe Community Church included readings, carol singing and wrapped up with a sermon.

Growing up, Jack had attended church services with his family every week. Pastor Reinhardt was a jovial fellow who would spread the Sunday newspaper on the pulpit and incorporate something that was happening locally or nationally into his message.

Jack had enjoyed attending, not only because the sermons were unique and interesting, but because he enjoyed seeing friends and extended family while there. His parents always had everyone over after the service. They'd grill out in the summer, and during the cold-weather months, they'd gather around the large kitchen table.

Once he'd moved to New York City, he'd been too busy to find a church home. For the past five years, the only times he'd been inside a church had been for weddings of family members and friends, with the occasional holiday appearance tossed into the mix.

He slanted a sideways glance at Melinda. She looked so pretty tonight in her emerald-green sweater with her red hair falling in soft waves around her shoulders.

As if she felt him looking at her, Melinda turned and flashed a smile before returning her attention to the pastor, who'd stepped to the pulpit.

Reaching over, he took her hand, pleased when she laced her fingers with his. A wave of contentment washed over Jack, and he settled in to listen to the message.

The minister had thinning brown hair and silver-rimmed glasses. His sharp-eyed gaze scanned the sanctuary. Then he smiled and began his sermon.

Jack hoped the man kept it short. That was one of the things he liked about the minister in his hometown. Pastor Reinhardt might take the time to add a unique flavor to his sermons, but he also got to the point.

Though he was sure a sunrise ceremony on the beach in Mexico had been memorable, the fact that Sam and Natalie had chosen a destination wedding in the first place still surprised Jack. He'd thought they would marry in the church they'd both attended since they were kids. Their decision only confirmed he hadn't known either one as well as he'd thought.

That would change, he vowed. He would make more time for his family. He would...

Melinda's head rested against his shoulder, and Jack decided the future could wait. He would savor the here and now.

Fifteen minutes later, the sermon concluded. At the start of the service, Pastor Shuck had encouraged them to move closer to open up more seating. Jack had been too focused on how good it felt to have Melinda pressed against him to pick up much of what had been said in the sermon. Though Jack felt fairly certain he'd heard the words *forgiveness* and *love* more than once.

Love.

He'd thought he loved Natalie, but now he had to wonder if you could truly love someone you didn't really know.

He slanted a glance at Melinda. He'd appreciated her support when he'd told her about Natalie and Sam and was glad she'd told him about her ex-boyfriend. They'd been barely more than strangers then, but had still felt comfortable confiding in each other.

Jack didn't trust many people, but he trusted Melinda.

At the airport, they'd been strangers. Tonight, they would enjoy their first Christmas Eve together.

Life, Jack thought, was definitely unpredictable.

When Melinda asked Jack if he wanted to spend Christmas Eve with her at her mom's house, she'd warned it wouldn't be anything fancy. There'd be simple fare—pizza, salad and breadsticks and homemade Christmas cookies for dessert.

Her alluding to certain traditions that he'd be expected to participate in might have raised a couple of alarms, but someone had interrupted them before he'd had a chance to ask for specifics.

Jack shrugged it off as he pulled into the drive. Melinda was beside him, looking as lovely as ever and smelling terrific.

The door opened before he could knock or Melinda could reach for the knob.

Both Rosie and Camryn stood there, identical Santa hats atop their heads. Broad, welcoming smiles lifted their lips.

"Merry Christmas." Rosie's voice boomed a welcome.

"I've got your hats." Camryn held up two Santa hats that matched hers and Rosie's.

Melinda reached for one, then handed it to Jack. "One of the traditions I mentioned." She offered a bright smile.

Melinda lifted her hat from Camryn's fingers. After putting it on, she heaved a melodramatic sigh. "If only it had a jingle bell."

Grateful for small favors, Jack slid on his, then smiled at Rosie. "Thank you for inviting me."

"I'm glad you could make it." Rosie gave his arm a squeeze. "I must say that Santa hat suits you."

Jack chuckled and decided if this was the worst of the traditions, he was in for a stellar evening.

Stepping aside, Rosie motioned them into the house, then took the sack of gifts Melinda had brought for her family. Jack had already purchased a special gift for Melinda, but after the invitation to Rosie's, he'd had to scramble to locate gifts for the others.

Rosie gestured with one hand. "Everyone is in the living room."

Jack took several steps, then paused at the sight of a photograph hanging on the wall. It was of a young Melinda—missing several teeth—surrounded by a group of boys, one of them her brother. With clear pride, she held up a sign proclaiming, "I'm the best."

Jack pointed to the photo. "What were you best at?"

Derek called out from the living room, where he was sitting with Shiloh, "Yeah, Melinda, tell the guy your big claim to fame."

"After all these years, you're still jealous a girl bested you and your friends," Melinda called back just as loudly.

Leaning close, Melinda spoke to Jack in a conspiratorial whisper. "It's very impressive."

"Now I'm really intrigued." Jack slid an arm around her and impulsively brushed a kiss across her hair.

"Keep it clean," Camryn warned, offering a cheeky smile. "There's a child in the house."

Melinda pulled back and made a big show of looking around, her eyes wide. "I don't see a child."

"If kissing isn't allowed, I'm not sure why I bothered hanging so much mistletoe." Rosie pointed to the greenery and red berries hanging just above the entrance to the living room. "There's another bunch on the way to the kitchen." She shot the two of them a wink. "Just in case you're interested."

Melinda chuckled. "Thanks, Mom."

"C'mon, Grandma." Camryn took Rosie's arm. "We've got work to do in the kitchen."

Once they were alone, Jack pointed to the photo. "I'm still curious what you were the best at."

"Spitting."

Jack blinked. "Say again?"

"I could spit farther than any boy I knew, including my brother and his friends." Melinda's lips curved in a smile that reminded him of a Cheshire cat. "They challenged me to a contest. I told them if I won, I would hold up a sign saying that, and they'd have to all be in the photo."

She gestured to the evidence of her victory.

Studying the picture, Jack couldn't keep from smiling. "What would have happened if you'd lost?"

"They said I'd have to make a sign that said something to the effect of 'I'm a dork,' or maybe it was 'I'm a dweeb.' I wasn't worried." Melinda waved a dismissive hand. "None of them could come close to spitting as far as me."

"I'm impressed." He tightened his hold and tugged her a little bit closer. "I didn't realize I was dating a celebrity."

"Well, now you know."

"Is it too late for a congratulatory kiss?"

"As long as you keep it short and sweet and save the more enthusiastic parts for later." She grinned. "We can't forget that there's a child in the house."

The kiss, short and sweet, stirred something within him. When she stepped from his embrace, Jack nearly protested, but she'd already slipped off her coat and was holding out a hand for his.

"My mom runs a tight ship, so now that we're here, things

should be getting started. I need at least one cup of mulled wine first. It smells yummy."

Jack had noticed the aroma of cinnamon and spices the second he'd stepped into the house.

"Mulled wine?" He recalled liking the taste, but it had been a long time since he'd had a cup. "The kind with apples or oranges?"

"Oranges and red wine."

"That's my favorite."

She inclined her head. "Would you have said that even if I'd said we were doing the white-wine-and-apples version?"

"No."

Melinda brushed his lips with hers. "I have to say there's something incredibly sexy about an honest guy."

He slipped his arms around her, but stepped back when Rosie called out, "Jack and Melinda, we're waiting in the kitchen for you. It's time to get to work."

He pulled his brows together, but kept his voice low. "I thought you said we were having pizza."

"We are." She grinned. "But another Kelly tradition is making the dessert of the evening...together."

Jack was surprised he could feel so relaxed in a home he'd never been in before, surrounded by a family that wasn't his and people he'd only recently met.

He'd gotten his mug of mulled wine, served the way he remembered, with orange slices floating on top, but had to drink it quickly.

Melinda hadn't been kidding when she'd said everyone helped make the dessert, which tonight was frosted sugar cookies.

"I prepared the dough yesterday," Rosie announced to the group gathered in the kitchen. The Santa hat remained atop her head as she slipped on an apron with A Recipe for Christmas Cheer stitched on the front.

"I prepared the icing." Camryn glanced around and smiled. "Which means my duty is done."

Derek slung an arm around his daughter. "Surely you'll help out your dear old dad?"

"Not a chance." Camryn slanted a glance at Shiloh. "Grandma assigned you and Dad to decorating. That's a super fun job."

"Your dad and I will rock the icing." Shiloh gave Derek an encouraging smile. "This is going to be a blast."

Jack glanced at Melinda. "That means you and I—"

"You and Melinda are in charge of cutting out the shapes," Rosie answered before Melinda had a chance.

"What about Carl?" Melinda asked, glancing at the older man standing next to her mom.

"I'm in charge of the Christmas music." Carl lifted his phone. "You let me know what you want to hear, and I'll play it for you."

"While he does that, I will be telling everyone what to do." Rosie chuckled, then added, "That's a particular strength of mine."

Soon, with Camryn's request of "Christmas Tree Farm" by Taylor Swift playing softly in the background, Jack and Melinda cut the prepared dough into stars, bells, snowflakes and Christmas trees.

Though Rosie supervised, she also took charge of the oven.

All too quickly, they were done baking the cookies.

"Do you need any help frosting?" Melinda asked her brother. "Jack and I are great decorators, especially when it comes to gingerbread houses."

She glanced at him, and they shared a smile.

"Thanks for the offer, but Shiloh and I have this under control," Derek told her.

"We've got big plans in terms of color for this next batch," Shiloh declared with a twinkle in her eye.

"I can't wait to see what you come up with," said Carl, who'd not only managed the music, but had also kept busy at the counter cutting out strings of paper snowflakes.

"Well, I can't wait to see how that snowflake chain turns out… and for you to show me how to do it," Shiloh told the older man.

Carl shot her a wink. "You just let me know when you're free, and we'll put scissors to paper."

"Mom…" Melinda pushed up from the table. "Since we're not needed in here, Jack and I are going into the living room to get everything set up for the game."

"Sounds good, honey." Rosie gave an absent wave. "Take some wine with you. You both did good work."

Jack admitted he was disappointed Derek and Shiloh hadn't needed help with frosting. Being part of the cookie detail had sounded more like fun than work.

There was something about this house and this family that put him at ease. Maybe it was the soft, warm lighting from the table lamps casting a golden glow. Maybe it was the clutter-free, but not perfectly staged, feel. Whatever it was, he liked being here…with Melinda and her family.

He followed Melinda into the living room. "What game are we setting up?"

"Actually, there's not much setup other than to make sure everything is tidy in here." Melinda reached down and folded a cotton throw that had slid off the sofa to the floor. "Camryn was in charge of compiling the questions this year."

"What kind of game are we talking about?" Jack set his and Melinda's cups on coasters.

When she dropped down on the sofa, he sat beside her.

"This year we're playing twenty Christmas questions." Melinda lifted her cup of mulled wine and took a sip.

"Sounds intense."

"Hardly." She laughed. "It's a lot of fun. We usually eat after that and then munch on cookies while we open gifts."

"The cookie making is a nice tradition."

"Yeah, it is." Melinda set down her cup and met his gaze. "I'm glad you came with me."

Jack smiled. "You know what tradition I really like?"

She shook her head.

"The mistletoe."

She glanced at the ceiling. "There's no mistletoe in here."

With some quick, sleight-of-hand magic, Jack produced a tiny sprig of mistletoe from his pocket and held it over her head.

Appearing delighted, Melinda grinned. "What am I going to do with you?"

"Kissing me would be a good start."

"Happy to oblige." Leaning over, Melinda had barely touched her lips to his when tromping feet signaled the arrival of the rest of the family.

"Who's ready to play twenty Christmas questions?" Derek called out.

Melinda offered Jack a rueful smile before turning to her brother. "Ready as we'll ever be."

CHAPTER SEVENTEEN

Carl brought his phone with him into the living room. After placing it on a side table, he took a seat next to Rosie on the love seat. Instead of taking requests as he had in the kitchen, he'd set a Christmas playlist, and sweet songs now filled the room.

When Derek, Shiloh and Camryn commandeered the sofa, Melinda and Jack resigned themselves to the chairs.

When Jack glanced at her, she mouthed, "Later," and his eyes lit up.

Yes, later, they could sit close, lie close, be together. A shiver of excitement coursed up her spine.

"I chose the questions." Camryn's gaze scanned the group. "If you don't like them, I don't want to hear any complaints." Everyone laughed. "Next year, you'll have your chance to choose."

Next year.

Melinda slanted a glance at Jack. Would she and Jack be together next Christmas?

Thankfully, she didn't have time to dwell on the possibility, because Camryn was ready for the game to begin.

"There are no right or wrong answers," the girl declared. "Each of you will answer every question."

"How many questions are there?" Shiloh asked.

"Five." Camryn lifted the first index card. "Shall we begin?"

After getting nods all around, Camryn read, "Eggnog or hot chocolate?"

Hot chocolate was the hands-down favorite until Camryn turned to Jack.

A twinkle filled Jack's eyes. "Will I be kicked out if I say eggnog?"

"You've got to be kidding." Derek grimaced. "Don't tell me you honestly prefer eggnog to hot chocolate?"

"Are you serious?" Camryn asked.

"Hey, it's okay if he likes eggnog." Melinda cast him a pitying glance. "It just means more hot chocolate for the rest of us."

That provoked laughter, and Camryn moved on to the next question. "What is your favorite holiday memory as a child?"

Melinda's mother, brother and niece had been part of her favorite memories, so Melinda found herself more interested in what Carl, Shiloh and Jack had to say.

Carl's best memory was being given a magic set when he was ten, while Shiloh's also involved a special gift—her first guitar at age nine.

Jack went last on this question, too.

"This is a it-happened-more-than-once memory." Jack's lips quirked upward. "My brother and I are close in age. In our family, we open gifts on Christmas morning. Sam and I would wait for our parents to go to bed on Christmas Eve. Once we were sure they were asleep, we would sneak downstairs and open our gifts. Then we would rewrap them and go back to bed."

"Why would you do that?" Shiloh asked, puzzlement furrowing her brow. "You'd be opening the gifts in the morning anyway."

Jack shrugged. "We were curious, and the presents were there."

Melinda could imagine two little boys—she pictured them in

matching pj's—sneaking downstairs and trying not to giggle. The image made her smile. "Did your parents ever find out what you were doing?"

"A nice way of asking if you ever got caught," Camryn said with a smirk.

Jack shook his head. "Not that we ever—"

"Your parents knew what was going on." Rosie spoke with utmost confidence. "I don't think there's a little boy or girl alive who can rewrap a package perfectly."

"If they knew, why didn't their parents say anything?" Camryn asked her grandmother.

"Because being aware they were doing it and not saying anything was part of the fun." Rosie pointed first to Derek and then to Melinda. "Just like I pretended to not know all those times when these two snuck out at night when they were in high school. I knew they weren't doing anything illegal or dangerous. If they had, I'd have busted them."

Camryn's eyes widened as she fixed her gaze on her dad. "You snuck out?"

Derek shot his mother a censuring glance.

Rosie simply took a sip of wine.

"I may have snuck out a few times." Derek smiled thinly. "Which means I know all the tricks, so don't you try it."

Camryn only laughed.

The next question, asking how they learned the truth about Santa, took longer.

Melinda was ready for pizza and hoped the answers to the final question came quickly.

"Last question." Camryn held up the white index card, then read, "Which do you prefer—giving or receiving?"

When the question finally came to Jack, he smiled. "I prefer to give."

No surprise, Melinda thought. She'd seen evidence of his giving spirit.

There was no chance for him to elaborate, because a loud ding sounded.

"Great job, Camryn." Rosie stood. "Let's all give our girl a big round of applause for the questions and for keeping us on track."

Melinda clapped and added a whistle that made her niece smile.

"The best part is that ding means that the pizza is ready." Rosie motioned for them to get up. "Come and get it."

Melinda wished Jack had been given time to say more, but then she realized that there was nothing he could say that she didn't already know.

The man was generous and caring. And she realized something else—she was falling in love with him.

~

After consuming two slices of pepperoni pizza, a bowl of salad and a breadstick, Melinda turned her thoughts to dessert. Christmas cookies and hot chocolate were the perfect combination.

When Rosie had apologized to Jack for not having any eggnog in the house, he'd flashed that heart-stopping smile and told her he liked hot cocoa, too.

Nibbling on a purple snowman cookie-Shiloh and Derek's attempt to jazz up the cookies—Melinda smiled and thought how nice it would be when she and Jack were alone...in her bed.

Camryn finished off the last of her silver bell and picked up a mug of hot chocolate. "What are you planning?"

Melinda blinked. "Planning?"

"You've got this secret-like smile on your face. The look in your eyes tells me you've got some kind of delicious plan brewing."

Thinking quickly, Melinda studied the huge dollop of homemade whipped cream on her niece's hot cocoa. "I'm planning to steal that whipped cream right off your—"

Lunging toward her niece with spoon outstretched, Melinda grinned when Camryn drew back.

"Get your own."

"I had my own. I ate it off the top. Now, I'm too comfortable to get up." Melinda sighed in contentment.

"Jack is nice."

Their gazes both shifted to where he and Derek were engaged in an animated conversation about sports.

"He is nice," Melinda agreed.

"Do you know he once wanted to be a magician?"

Melinda shot her niece a skeptical look. "Jack a magician? Where did you hear that?"

"He was telling Carl all about this magic kit he had when he was twelve and how he would practice all these tricks." Camryn shook her head and this time used her spoon to scoop up the whipped cream. "Carl liked talking to him. I could tell. That made Grandma happy."

"Did it?"

"She likes Carl. A lot." Camryn sipped thoughtfully. "Just the way you like Jack."

"Jack and I are friends."

"I have lots of friends. None of them looks at me the way he looks at you." Camryn put down her spoon. "Not one of them kisses me either."

"You're making something out of nothing." Still, when Jack glanced over and gave her what she was beginning to think of as their secret smile, Melinda blushed.

Later, when Jack was helping Carl tend to the fire in the hearth, Derek strolled up to Melinda and slung an arm around her shoulders.

"How's it going?" she asked.

"It's going well. How's it for you?"

"This evening has been nice. Relaxed." Derek pointed his beer bottle toward Jack. "You've got a good one there. Fits right in."

"Camryn said he and Carl bonded over magic. Apparently, Jack had this thing for magic tricks when he was in middle school."

Just thinking of Jack performing such tricks made her smile.

"He and I talked football. And hockey. And you."

Melinda had been simply nodding along, then stopped. "Me? What about me?"

"He asked what you were like as a kid. Apparently, the spitting thing had him wondering." Derek gave her a squeeze, then dropped his arm. "I assured him that I haven't seen you spit in years. It's not like something you do on a regular basis."

"Ah, thank you for that." Melinda spoke in a droll tone, but was unable to keep from smiling.

"Basically, I said I think you make a good pair, and I hope he sticks around."

Melinda groaned aloud. "You did not say that."

"I did." Derek took another swig of beer. "Because that's how I feel."

"He's only here over the holidays, Derek."

Derek inclined his head. "You don't think you'll stay in touch?"

"I don't know. We only met last week." It was something that Melinda had to keep reminding herself every time she found herself wondering if they could build something lasting together. "He—"

Melinda stopped speaking when Rosie, with Carl standing next to her, clapped her hands.

Now that the fire burned brightly in the hearth, Jack crossed the room to stand beside Melinda.

"Great job on the fire," she whispered.

"Thanks."

He might have said more, and she definitely would have said

more, but her mother commanded center stage. "For those of you who haven't had a cookie, or enough cookies, grab some now. We're opening gifts in ten minutes."

Camryn pushed up from her seat and motioned for Jack to take her place. "I want another cookie. Can I get either of you one?"

Melinda shook her head. "I'm good."

Jack considered. "I could eat another."

Camryn flashed a smile. "Coming up."

Instead of immediately dropping down beside her on the love seat, Jack hesitated. "Is there anything I can do to help with the gifts?"

Melinda gestured to where her mother and Carl were going through the wrapped packages and putting them into piles. "My mom has always been the one to separate the gifts. Even when I begged to help as a kid, she insisted that, as the oldest, it was her job."

"She's letting Carl help."

That fact hadn't escaped Melinda's notice. "Probably because he's older than her."

Even though that made sense and was absolutely true, Melinda didn't think that was why.

"This has been a good evening," Jack said.

"If all those packages are any indication," Melinda smiled, "the best is yet to come."

The gift unwrapping at the end of the evening ended up being a fun, relaxed affair.

The tradition in the Kelly household was they started with the oldest, then eventually got to the youngest.

"I think it's reverse age discrimination." Camryn pouted even as her eyes sparkled.

"I think it's reverse something," Melinda pointed to the stack of packages in front of Camryn, "when you've got five gifts to every one of mine."

Camryn glanced down, then grinned. "Forget I said anything."

Carl started off, exclaiming over gifts from Derek, Camryn and Rosie.

He opened the box from Melinda, then looked up and smiled broadly. "I've never had a Saint Paddy's Day bow tie."

Showing off the contents for all to see, he shot another warm smile at Melinda. "Thank you. I love it."

"There's one gift left." Camryn pointed to a square box on the floor at Carl's feet.

"This one is from Jack." Carl smiled at Jack. "You didn't have to get me anything."

That had Melinda remembering that Jack had brought in his own sack of gifts.

"It's Christmas." Jack gestured to the package. "Unwrap it and let me know what you think."

From the paper that boasted handwritten script incorporating famous holiday quotes and seasonal greetings, Melinda knew the gift had come from Yule Books.

"The Life and Afterlife of Harry Houdini." A smile blossomed on Carl's lips. "This is a wonderful, thoughtful gift."

"I read it and enjoyed it," Jack told him. "I thought that you, as a fellow magician, might enjoy it as well."

"I can't wait to get started." Carl's weathered hands clasped the book. "Thank you."

By the time it was Melinda's turn, she couldn't help wondering what Jack had gotten her. She hoped it wasn't anything too personal. On the other hand, she hoped it *was* personal.

He'd seemed to like her gift—the *Star Wars* figure he'd admired when they'd visited Memory Lane.

Melinda didn't recognize the wrapping paper as coming from

a specific shop in Holly Pointe. It wasn't a large package, and by the time she tore off the red and white candy-striped paper and shiny red bow to find a small white box, she still wasn't sure what could be inside.

"What is it?" Camryn pressed, leaning forward from her spot on the floor beside Melinda.

"If I can get this open, I'll tell you." The top finally opened, allowing Melinda to see what was inside. "It's a candle." She smiled at Jack, then read the description. "Cozy Fireplace."

"There's a note with it." Camryn picked up the small piece of paper that had fluttered to the ground when Melinda had pulled out the candle.

Melinda read the words silently to herself. *A crackling fire brings warmth to a room. You bring warmth to my heart.*

She turned to Jack and kissed him lightly on the lips. "Thank you."

Camryn looked from Melinda to Jack. "What does the note say?"

"Something just for me." Melinda carefully folded the note and put it in her pocket before her gaze returned to Jack.

At that moment, time seemed to stand still. He had transformed a simple moment into a memory to cherish.

When her eyes locked on his, heat flowed through her body like an awakened river. Once he took her home, they would light a fire in the hearth and create even more beautiful memories.

CHAPTER EIGHTEEN

Once the wrapping paper and gift bags had been cleared away, Rosie insisted on making Peppermint Mochas for everyone.

When she handed Jack his, she smiled. "I have a wonderful Eggnog Latte recipe. Next year, we'll have that instead."

Melinda started to say Jack would likely not be around next year, but the thought made her sad, so she took a sip of the decadent mocha instead.

Once everyone had a drink in hand, with Carl standing at her side, Rosie cleared her throat. "As you all are aware, other than my family, the diner has been my priority for most of my life." Looking attractive in a rose velour sweater, she gripped Carl's hand. "I wish I could have been there more for you kids when you were growing up."

"I think we turned out just fine," Derek told her. "Despite running the streets of big, bad Holly Pointe by ourselves all those years."

"Don't forget hanging out with all the unsavory people in the diner," Melinda piped up. "Like Mr. Hildegard, the retired grade school teacher."

"While refilling salt and pepper shakers which," Derek paused for effect, "I believe was a clear violation of child labor laws."

Rosie chuckled, and her tense expression relaxed. "I'm proud of you both. And of you, Camryn."

"Thanks, Grandma." Camryn blew Rosie a kiss. "Love you lots."

"Love you back, sweetie." Rosie turned to Carl, and a soft smile lifted her lips before she refocused on the others in the room. "Like I said, work has pretty much been my life. Lately, I find myself wanting more."

Melinda shifted in her seat. When her mother had begun speaking, she'd thought her mom might be ready to announce some changes to the diner. Now, she had the feeling it was something much more personal.

"Do you want to tell them?" Carl asked. "Or do I get the pleasure?"

Rosie laughed and linked her arm with his. "Why don't you do the honors? I'm a bit tired of hearing myself talk."

"I could listen to you all evening," Carl said gallantly, then faced the family. "I asked this wonderful woman to marry me, and she made me very happy by saying yes."

"Grandma." Camryn was the first to react, jumping up and crossing to Rosie and Carl. "Congratulations."

"Thank you, sweetheart." Rose hugged her granddaughter and planted a kiss on the top of her head.

"Congrats." Derek kissed his mom's cheek and shook Carl's hand. "I'm happy for both of you."

Melinda hugged her mother hard. "Congratulations. I love seeing you so happy."

Despite the tightness in her chest, the words slid out smoothly. She did want her mother to be happy. That's what she'd always wanted.

Releasing her hold on her mother, Melinda gave Carl a hug. "I know you'll take good care of her."

Carl glanced at Rosie with love shining strong in his eyes. "We'll take good care of each other."

Jack now stood beside Melinda. "Congratulations to you both. I know you'll be very happy together."

Pink colored Rosie's cheeks, and her hands trembled as she pushed back a strand of hair and glanced around the room. "I was so nervous about telling you."

"She was," Carl agreed, placing a hand on her shoulder. "I told her that she had nothing to worry about."

"Nothing to worry about at all." Melinda met her mother's gaze and spoke in a hearty tone. "I believe this announcement calls for champagne, don't you?"

"Can I have a glass?" Camryn turned pleading eyes to her father. "Please, Daddy. This is a big deal."

Derek hesitated for only a second, then turned to Melinda. "Half a glass."

Jack looked at Melinda. "I assume you have a bottle on hand."

Though he'd spoken to Melinda, Rosie answered. "There's a bottle in the fridge…" Rosie began.

"I'm aware, Mom." Melinda smiled brightly. "And just so you know, I'm bringing out the good crystal wineglasses. It's not every day you get engaged."

"Thank you, sweetheart." Rosie blinked back tears. "I can't tell you how much I appreciate you making this so special for Carl and me."

Jack stayed in the living room for another minute to speak with Carl before slipping into the kitchen after Melinda. He found her facing the sink, her hands on the counter.

Not wanting to startle her, he kept his tone light and spoke softly. "Having trouble finding the champagne?"

"I know where it is. I just needed a minute."

Melinda turned with a bright smile. Jack wasn't fooled. At that moment, he wanted nothing more than to enfold her in his arms and do whatever he could to comfort and soothe.

For now, he remained where he was, sensing comfort wasn't what Melinda needed. She had things to work out in her head. He hoped she understood she didn't need to do that alone. He was here and wanted to help.

"I'm sensing this announcement came as a complete surprise." He placed a hand on her arm. "Are you okay?"

Her smile never wavered. "Why wouldn't I be? My mother just got engaged, and she's over the moon."

"Your words say one thing, but I can tell that smile isn't genuine."

A stricken look crossed her face. "Do you think anyone else noticed?"

"No. You're very convincing." No longer able to resist, he pulled her into his arms and held her tight.

After several long seconds, she pulled back.

"I can't believe she agreed to marry him, Jack." Worry filled Melinda's hazel eyes, and her voice shook with emotion. "They haven't even been dating a year."

"If they'd dated since last Christmas, would that be enough?"

Her brows pulled together. "I don't understand."

"If they'd been dating for a year, would you feel better about them becoming engaged?"

"I wish I could say yes." Melinda raked a hand through her hair. "Honestly, I don't know."

Jack rested his back against the counter and forced an offhand tone. "Is it that you don't like Carl?"

"He's not the kind of guy I pictured her with." Melinda blew out a breath. "At the Independence Day celebration, he wore this red, white and blue tie that flashed and a hat that played 'You're a Grand Old Flag.' That's why I knew he'd love the Saint Paddy's Day bow tie."

Though he couldn't resist smiling at the image that popped into his head, Jack quickly sobered. "Are you saying he's too silly?"

"My mom isn't silly. She's pragmatic. She focuses on work and getting things done. Or, that's how she's been." Melinda flung out her hands in frustration. "Now, all of a sudden, she's taking off time to be his magic show assistant at the resort and talking about, well, wanting to take time to smell the roses."

"Those are..." Jack paused. Those were Rosie's choices and certainly understandable ones, but Melinda didn't need him to remind her of something she already knew.

"My mom's second marriage was to a guy she supported for ten years before kicking him to the curb."

Now, Jack thought, they were getting to the heart of Melinda's reservations. His father had once told him that when a person was struggling with a decision, it wasn't that they didn't know the answer, it was that they needed someone to listen so they could talk through it in their own head.

It appeared that's what Melinda was doing now.

"Was your stepdad silly like Carl?"

Melinda shook her head. "He was controlling. At least he tried to control my mom. You can imagine how that went over. I was surprised they remained married for as long as they did."

Silence fell between them.

After a moment, Jack ventured, "Your mom has had a tough road when it comes to men. I mean, first your father dies and leaves her with two little kids. Then she marries someone who isn't right for her. Now, she meets Carl."

Melinda's gaze laser-focused on him. "What do you think of him?"

It would be so easy to say the first response that came to mind —that what he thought about Carl didn't matter—but he did have an opinion, and it seemed wrong not to voice it when she'd asked him to.

"I don't know him well, but he was telling me how he likes making balloon animals not only for kids but also for adults because there's not enough joy in life. He believes if you can make someone's day with a smile or a kind word, you should do it."

"You think he's a good man."

"I believe he is."

Melinda inhaled a deep breath, then let it out slowly and pointed. "Want to get the champagne? I'll grab the glasses. Then we'll go in and toast the happy couple."

~

Melinda hadn't planned to be in Holly Pointe on Christmas Day, so she hadn't purchased a new dress for the Mistletoe Ball. Luckily, she had one in her closet that no one had yet seen.

Last year, before the ball was officially canceled, replaced by something much more casual, she'd gone shopping. When she'd picked up the dress to try on, the clerk had told her the shimmering gold gown "exuded elegance and sophistication." Melinda didn't know about that. She only knew she'd fallen in love with it the second she'd seen the halter neckline embellished with sparkling crystals.

The fitted bodice cinched at the waist, accentuating her figure, while the full skirt gracefully flowed to the floor.

Melinda did her own hair, working on the half-up, half-down style until it looked as if she'd visited a salon. Artfully applied makeup and bright red lipstick completed the picture.

She smiled into the mirror, a single thought circling in her brain.

Tonight, she would attend the Mistletoe Ball. Not alone, or with a friend, but with Jack.

~

For this year's Mistletoe Ball, the large barn at Grace Hollow had been transformed into an Enchanted Winter Wonderland, with glistening white and silver decorations adorning every corner. Snowflake-shaped chandeliers cast a magical glow over the dance floor.

Twinkling fairy lights, draped like icicles, illuminated the room, adding to the romantic atmosphere. Melinda waited while Jack checked their coats.

From everything she'd seen so far, the decorating committee had done a fabulous job of combining an Enchanted Winter Wonderland theme with this year's Christmas Moon.

The entrance to the ballroom resembled a moonlit pathway with white fabric creating an ethereal tunnel. In the tunnel were fairy lights, strategically placed lanterns and scattered silver glitter to mimic a starry night sky.

The women stepping into the tunnel wore exquisite floor-length dresses in rich jewel tones and shimmering fabrics adorned with sequins, beads and lace. The men who weren't wearing tuxedos wore sharp suits complemented by polished shoes and perfectly knotted ties.

Jack, resplendent in a dark tuxedo he'd rented for the evening, appeared at her side and took her arm. "Ready for the tunnel walk?"

"I am."

This year, a live orchestra took center stage, serenading the guests with enchanting melodies of classic holiday tunes. The music enticed guests to sway to the rhythm of the music on a dance floor where a gobo light projector cast moon-shaped patterns on the surface.

The scene spread out before Melinda was a far cry from last year's Rockin' Reindeer Bash with its red and white checkerboard dance floor and a teenage DJ spinning the hits. Though that had been fun, too, Melinda recalled. It was a time when the entire community had come together.

Once they were in the main ballroom, they drank cocktails with names like Moonlight Kiss and Lunar Bliss. They kissed under sprigs of mistletoe that had been strategically suspended from doorways and arches throughout the ballroom.

They laughed and talked with friends and family. They danced and kissed some more.

When Jack held her on the dance floor and they swayed to enchanting melodies, Melinda found herself struck by a heartfelt wish that this would never end.

"I meant to ask you earlier—what's with the celestial props?" Jack asked as they danced past a photo booth where guests could take pictures under a large moon-shaped backdrop.

"There's a full moon tonight," she told him. "Remember, when it falls on Christmas, which it rarely does, it's known as a Christmas Moon. It's supposed to represent a time of new beginnings."

"New beginnings?" Jack grinned. "Appropriate."

Melinda only smiled at the puzzling comment and rested her head against his broad chest.

When the song ended, instead of remaining on the dance floor, Jack took her hand. "Come with me."

"Where are we going?"

"Just over here."

Over here ended up being a spot by the windows. They stood hand in hand, overlooking a vast field blanketed in freshly fallen snow. The moon hung high in the sky and cast a soft, ethereal glow over the pristine white landscape.

In silence, they took a moment to absorb the breathtaking beauty in front of them. The snow-covered trees and hills in the distance seemed to blend seamlessly with the wintry night sky.

Then, in perfect synchronicity, they turned toward each other. Jack's gaze met hers, and when his arms slid around her and he lowered his head to kiss her, Melinda embraced the magic of the moment.

When the kiss finally ended, she stepped back and smiled.

"I have a gift for you." Jack's lips curved, and his eyes seemed to glow in the dim light.

"We already exchanged gifts last night."

"Are you saying you won't accept another?"

"I'm not saying that at all." She laughed and glanced around. "Where is it?"

Reaching into his pocket, he grabbed a small object, then held it out to her.

Melinda took the key chain, turning it over in her hands. There was something familiar about the odd shape, but she couldn't place it or make sense of the tiny heart with the broken line that twisted and turned until it reached the edge of the shape.

She looked up in puzzlement. "What is this?"

"That's the shape of the state of New York," he explained. "The heart is where JFK airport is located, and the line is the air route to Mexico."

"You gave it to me to remind me of where we first met." Suddenly, Jack's comment on the dance floor made sense. "Where it all began."

"I wanted you to have it as a reminder of that day at JFK and as a symbol of the new."

She inclined her head. "Our new...friendship?"

"I think what's between us is more than friendship, but we can talk about that at another time. I want you to go with me to Mexico, Melinda." He held up a hand as if to stop her from talking before he could say what he wanted to say. "We already have our tickets for the twenty-ninth. While the resort we were planning to stay at is fully booked, I found one even nicer that can accommodate us."

"It sounds wonderful, but..." Her teeth found her bottom lip.

Jack tugged her to him, his husky voice wrapping around her heart. "Tell me why you're hesitating."

"I could barely afford the other resort," she admitted. "The one you booked is likely out of my price range."

"My treat." When she opened her mouth to protest, he pushed ahead. "I can afford it, Melinda. You've given me a wonderful Christmas here in Holly Pointe. Please let me reciprocate and show you a wonderful time in Mexico."

Melinda could picture it. Sun. Sand. Jack.

"Okay." Melinda's heart picked up speed. "I'll go with you on one condition."

She could almost see Jack brace himself.

"We have to share a room. That will save money." Leaning close, she kissed him. "And I'm thinking it wouldn't be half as enjoyable a trip if we have to go our separate ways at night."

"If you insist." Jack tried, but he couldn't seem to keep a straight face. "We'll do it your way."

"I think we'll both be happy with that decision." Her gaze turned to the moon. "Someone once told me that often the best gifts are the ones we never expect."

"You never expected the trip."

"I never expected you." Melinda cupped her hands around his neck. "You, Jack McPherson, are my best gift this Christmas."

CHAPTER NINETEEN

Melinda woke the next morning to sunshine streaming through the window. She rolled over, expecting to find a warm male body next to her.

Jack had been there when she'd finally fell asleep, after first exploring every delicious inch of his body. He'd been there when she'd awakened during the night to the feel of his palm sliding up her back.

They'd made love again before falling into an exhausted slumber. Melinda had never been with someone who made her feel the way that Jack did. They didn't just have sex—they made love. She realized now the difference was monumental.

This time, when she reached for him, she discovered that she was alone. The covers on his side of the bed had been carefully turned back. On her side, the duvet that often ended up on the floor because of her restlessness had been tucked around her.

Could he have left?

The thought had her bolting upright, the covers falling to her waist and her skin turning to gooseflesh. She could have nestled back under the deliciously warm covers, but hopped out of bed instead.

Her feet had barely hit the hardwood when she heard his voice coming from the direction of the kitchen. Relief surged as she grabbed her robe from the hook on the back of the door. Pulling it on, she cinched the belt tight, took a few steps and listened.

A few seconds of financial mumbo jumbo confirmed what she'd thought—he was on a business call.

Deciding to give him space to do what he needed to do, Melinda showered, slapped on some makeup and then dressed. By the time she was ready to face the world, he was still on the call.

After taking a moment to make the bed and straighten up the bathroom, Melinda decided her system couldn't wait one second more for caffeine.

Leaving her shoes off, she made her way to the kitchen. Melinda decided she must not have been creeping as soundlessly as she'd thought, because Jack turned when she reached the doorway.

He held up a finger. "Del, could you hold just a second?"

After apparently receiving assent, he placed the person on hold.

"Good morning." He offered her a warm smile. "I hope I didn't wake you."

Melinda shook her head. "Go ahead and finish your call. I just need coffee."

"I made a pot for us." He gestured with his head toward the phone. "I should be off in ten to fifteen. Does that work for you?"

"No problem."

"Thanks." Jack took the call off mute. "Del, I'm back. Let's go through those figures one more time."

Only then did Melinda notice the pad of paper and pen on the table. The sheet in front of Jack was filled with notes and figures.

While he focused on the conversation, Melinda paused with her hand on the coffeepot and let her gaze linger on him. When they'd left the ball last night, they'd swung by Reindeer Rest to pick up a change of clothes and whatever else he'd need this morning.

She wasn't sure how a cream-colored sweater, jeans and boots could look even more delectable on him than a tux, but the casual look did it all for her.

He did it all for her.

Intelligent, kind, generous and fun, he was everything she'd been looking for in a man. The funny thing was, she hadn't even been looking when their paths had crossed.

Smiling at the irony and thinking of the dating-site failures she'd experienced in Burlington had her shaking her head as she filled a large mug with coffee.

By the time she finished replying to a text from Faith telling her she'd given birth to a healthy baby boy at eleven-twenty last night, Jack was off the phone.

"If you need to make more calls, I'm cool with it." Melinda lifted her red mug. "I've got my coffee. I'm in a toasty-warm house on a snowy day. All is good."

"I'm done for today." Jack moved to the counter and refilled his own mug. "Since I'll be away from the office longer than I initially intended, there were a few things I needed to discuss with my partner."

"Your voice changes when you talk business."

A startled look crossed his face. "It does?"

Melinda nodded. "There's an excitement underlying all the business stuff. I wasn't sure what you were talking about, but I could tell you loved it. You were in the zone."

"I do love it," he admitted.

"I hope one day I can find something that fills me with that same excitement." She met his gaze. "Finding one's passion is a gift."

He placed a reassuring hand on her arm. "Give it time."

"I'm thirty." Melinda gave a little laugh. "You'd think if I was going to find it, I'd have done so by now."

"Colonel Sanders didn't start cooking and selling his famous fried chicken until he was in his forties. Vera Wang didn't enter the world of fashion design until she was forty. Julia Child worked in advertising before discovering her passion for cooking. Frank McCourt worked as a teacher. He was in his sixties before he published—"

"Enough. Enough." Melinda laughed and held up a staying hand. "I get the picture. I can't believe you had all those examples in your back pocket."

"I possess a wealth of what some might call useless information," he joked before his expression turned serious. "If you ever want to brainstorm possibilities…"

"I know just who to come to." She stepped close. Unable to keep from touching him, she ran her hands up his sweater front. "What would you like to do today?"

"You're the Holly Pointe expert." Leaning over, Jack nuzzled her neck. "You tell me."

What would she like to do? Melinda considered mentioning returning to bed, but consoled herself that that would still be there tonight. So would he.

Last night, he'd told her he would remain in Holly Pointe with her until they left for New York for their flight to Mexico.

Three more days. Three more nights.

Then, Mexico.

Before that happened, there was more to show him here. Much more.

"I was on a committee charged with coming up with after-Christmas activities."

"*After*-Christmas activities?" Mild interest flickered in his blue depths.

"Yes. After." She smiled. "If you think about it, many visitors stay a couple of days after Christmas before heading home. Some remain in Holly Pointe through the end of the year. We wanted to offer activities that they could enjoy, not only before Christmas, but after as well."

One of the hands he'd rested on her waist slid under the hem of her sweater. He kept it there as he waited for her to continue.

Her skin heated beneath his touch. Melinda cleared her throat. "We, ah, came up with ten different scavenger-hunt-type activities for visitors to choose from."

"How do visitors even know these activities exist?"

"Just like they know about all the others—the Holly Pointe app." Melinda couldn't stop the smile as she thought of the difference the app had made in tourism. Visitors could easily keep track of what was going on in town no matter when they visited Holly Pointe.

"Are you serious?" Surprise flickered across his face. "I haven't heard anything about an app."

"Making everyone aware of the app's existence is something we're working on."

Jack gave a thoughtful nod. "Since I don't have the app, why don't you tell me the activities, and we can choose one?"

"Do you want to hear all of them, or just the ones that have been added to the app?"

"Some were left off?"

"Five went on, and five were left off." Melinda made a face. "My favorite, the one I called Santa's Secret, didn't make the cut."

There had been a lot of discussion between committee members on which events to include on the app. In the end, the majority had decided to promote only the top five.

"I'll start by giving you five." Melinda raised one hand and began counting off on her fingers. "Gingerbread Man Hunt. Cutouts of gingerbread men are hidden in different spots around town. Participants are encouraged to find them all."

Jack's hand slid a little farther up her side.

Melinda sucked in a breath, but his fingers stopped. At least for the moment.

"Then there's one called Christmas Tree Trail, where participants identify a sequence of trees or landmarks that will lead them to a hidden holiday-themed treasure."

Jack inclined his head. "What's the treasure?"

Her lips curved. "I'm not telling."

His hand moved up another inch.

After drawing a shaky breath, Melinda continued. "Another one is the Holiday Character Hunt. It's a lot like the Gingerbread Man Hunt, except you search for cutouts of holiday characters, like elves, reindeer or snowmen, in unexpected places."

"That sounds very similar to the other."

"That's what I said. I wanted my favorite to be on there instead, but I was overruled." Melinda shrugged.

"I'm sorry. Being overruled is always frustrating." He kissed her softly as his hand slid upward another inch.

She shivered, liking the direction his hand was headed.

"The fourth is Twinkling Lights, where participants find clusters of twinkling holiday lights or specific light arrangements."

Jack gave a grudging nod. "That one is at least different from the others."

"Ready for the last one?"

"Can't wait."

"Seasonal Word Search."

"Wow," he drawled. "Sounds exciting."

"It could be." She smiled. "Actually, it's one of my favorites."

"How does it work?"

"Clues lead participants to signs with holiday-related words."

"I can see where that might be interesting." Jack studied her for a long moment. "Your committee went to a lot of trouble putting these together."

"It wasn't my committee, it was Kate's. I was just a member."

"Knowing you, I'm sure you had a large hand in all of this." His gaze turned curious. "You said your favorite didn't get selected. Tell me about that one."

"I called it Santa's Secret Message. I created three messages—riddles, really—that eventually lead to a location where participants find a heartwarming message from Santa."

"A heartwarming message."

"Very heartwarming." Melinda expelled a sigh. "I think that was part of the problem. Since Christmas would be over, the other committee members felt like this would be something that fit better before Christmas than after."

"I get that." Jack offered her a sympathetic smile. "Still, I wish I could have seen what you came up with."

"We can still do it." Melinda spoke quickly. "But I need to warn you. Since I know where the clues lead, you'll be on your own in terms of deciphering them."

"You put the clues out there even though Santa's Secret Message wasn't chosen?"

She lifted one shoulder, let it drop. "I figured Camryn and her friends might get a kick out of playing."

"Let's do it."

"Right now?" When he hesitated, she added, "If you have more work to do, we can head out after you finish."

"I have a bit of business to take care of before we go." His eyes grew dark as his hand slid the rest of the way up and unclasped her bra. "But what I have in mind doesn't have a thing to do with finance."

Once Melinda was back in bed with Jack, she hadn't wanted to leave. But she was eager to discover what he thought of the scavenger hunt she'd devised. So, after one more kiss, she rolled out of bed and quickly dressed for the second time that day.

Snow continued to fall, as it had off and on all morning, but there had been little additional accumulation. As she and Jack had dressed for the weather, Melinda barely noticed the cold as she stepped outside.

Jack slanted a sideways glance in her direction. "Do we walk or drive to the first clue?"

"You tell me." She offered an enigmatic smile. "I texted the clue to you."

Without needing to glance at his phone, he recited, "'Follow the path of twinkling lights to where Santa's message takes its flight. At the place where candy canes align, you'll find a hint that's quite divine.'"

"You've got a great memory." Melinda cocked her head. "Now, tell me where you think you'll find this hint. That should tell you if we should drive or walk."

"'Candy canes align.'" His brows pulled together as he thought for several seconds, then his eyes lit up. "The Candy Cane Christmas House has candy canes lined up on both sides of the walkway leading to the house."

Melinda only smiled.

"I think if that's where we're going, we should drive."

Mary Pierson's house wasn't far in a car, but it would have taken a while to walk. Once they reached the home, Melinda got out when Jack did, but made no move to leave the side of the car.

"'At the place where candy canes align, you'll find a hint,'" Jack murmured to himself.

Without glancing at Melinda, he strode down the walkway leading to the porch, scanning both sides where the candy canes were placed. He finally came to a stop near the porch.

Turning back to Melinda, he motioned for her. "I found the next clue."

Melinda sauntered up the sidewalk, hoping she hadn't made this scavenger hunt too easy. When she got there, he was reading the clue that had been painted in a flowery font onto a small cutout Santa figure: "'Now onward to where the reindeer roam, where the scent of pine and evergreen roam. At Santa's Mailbox, pause and see the next part of this message, merry and free.'"

"I think I know where the reindeers are housed." Jack narrowed his gaze on Melinda. "Is that where I'll find the next clue?"

"This wouldn't be any fun if I gave you the answers."

The stables were located several miles outside of Holly Pointe. They were almost there when Jack slowed the car.

"It's not going to be this far out." He slanted her a sideways glance. "Not when most visitors stay in town."

She saw the question in his eyes, heard it in his voice, but only shrugged.

He blew out a breath. "We're almost to the stables, so I might as well check."

Melinda only settled back in the heated seat. She loved spending time with Jack, but realized this hunt would be more fun if she didn't already know the answers, if they could be truly searching together.

Once they were at the stables, Melinda remained in the car while Jack did what she thought of as a quick, scouting operation.

When he returned to the car, his cheeks were red from the cold.

"Came up empty?" was all she said.

"There's pine all around, and this is where the reindeer roam, but there's no Santa's Mailbox anywhere. At least not where I could see."

"It would have to be out in the open where anyone could see," Melinda said in response to his questioning glance.

"That's what I thought." He turned the car around and headed back into town. "The 'reindeer roam' thing throws me."

"At this time of year, you can find reindeer most everywhere in Holly Pointe."

Jack nodded.

Melinda could almost see his analytic brain considering and discarding various possibilities.

"Think back to where you last saw a reindeer," she prompted.

"In town. There were two of them out in front of that house— I can't remember what it was called..."

"The Bromley mansion," Melinda supplied.

"They were tethered there, but they weren't roaming." Still, he turned in that direction. "I'm going to check it out."

They found a parking spot in front of Yule Books, then got out and walked to the two-story Queen Anne home.

The streets were filled with shoppers taking advantage of the after-Christmas sales.

"There it is," a woman exclaimed in a loud voice. "A reindeer."

Jack and Melinda weren't the only ones who turned as a woman in her fifties pointed to a cutout of a reindeer positioned in front of the Busy Bean.

"Now all we need is an elf and a snowman," she announced to her friends.

"I bet they're doing the Holiday Character Hunt," Melinda told Jack, pleased that the scavenger hunts had attracted some interest.

"The clue mentions greenery and the scent of pine." Jack gestured to the doors and windows of the mansion that displayed gorgeous evergreen wreaths. "If you count that cardboard reindeer, we could be in the right place."

"You could," Melinda said in a noncommittal voice.

"You're not going to help me at all, are you?"

"You wouldn't want me to give anything away." Melinda might not have known Jack long, but she knew he didn't want things handed to him.

"You're right." His gaze scanned the front of the mansion before he walked around it, with Melinda trailing behind him, trying her best to keep a smile from her face.

For some reason, she was reminded of the hiding game she

and her brother had often played as children. They'd hide an object and then direct their sibling to it by saying, "You're hot," or "You're getting cold."

Part of her wished she could play that game with Jack now, because as he rounded the back of the mansion, he was getting very, very cold.

"No mailbox," Jack decreed, "so this can't be the space."

His gaze returned to the house, to the evergreen and the scent of pine, then to the reindeer cutout in front of the Busy Bean.

"Can a clue function for more than one game?"

Melinda smiled. "That would be efficient."

A grin split his face. "I know where we can find the next clue."

"Really?" She pretended to look around. "Because I don't see Santa's Mailbox."

"It's inside the Busy Bean," he told her, striding to the entrance to the coffee shop and flinging open the door. "I saw it the first time I stopped in there."

Santa's Mailbox stood near the fireplace. Painted in festive red, the mailbox sported hand-painted snowflakes and holly leaves. A miniature wreath made from real pinecones and adorned with a red velvet bow graced the post.

"There it is." Jack pointed, then strode over to the box, stuck his hand inside and pulled out a sheet of paper. Glancing down at it, he smiled triumphantly. "I've got the next clue."

"Great job."

"I still don't get the pinecone reference—"

When Melinda gestured with her head toward the mailbox, and he studied it more closely.

When his gaze lingered on the wreath decorated with pinecones, his lips curved. "I see it now."

"You're on the right track," Kenny called out, then turned to Melinda. "Camryn and several of her friends were in earlier, following the same clues."

"Sounds as if we're not the only ones having fun with this," Jack told Melinda.

"Are you?" Melinda asked. "Having fun?"

Jack slung an arm around her shoulders. "I could be doing nothing and still be having fun, as long as I'm with you."

CHAPTER TWENTY

After solving the last clue and discovering Santa's Secret Message, Melinda and Jack headed to Rosie's for lunch.

Bethany took their order, brought their food and kept their cups filled with coffee.

"I haven't seen my mother. Is she in the back?" Melinda asked Bethany when they'd finished eating and Rosie still hadn't appeared.

"She was in this morning." Bethany cast quick glances at her other tables. "Once the lunch rush died down, she left, but I heard her say she'd be back."

"Okay, thanks." Melinda turned back to Jack. "I know you said you enjoyed the scavenger hunt, but tell me honestly, what did you think of that last clue?"

When Melinda had put together the game, she'd worried that the ending came too easy and that some might find Santa's Secret Message kind of schmaltzy.

"The last clue was definitely the easiest." Once again, Jack recited from memory, "'You're on the trail and doing great. Now head to where you can skate. Look for frosty friends upon the ice and discover Santa's Secret Message, oh-so-nice.'"

"Way too easy?"

"It was easy," Jack agreed, then offered a reassuring smile. "The way I see it, whoever participates will be in the homestretch at that point. They'll want easy."

"You think?"

"I do." As if he sensed she wanted more, Jack continued. "It was obvious the location was Spring Lake, but the 'frosty friends upon the ice' threw me, until I saw the snowman. He wasn't really 'on the ice,' but close enough."

"What did you think of Santa's Secret Message?"

"'Celebrate today, because it's a gift that can never be unwrapped again.'" Jack took a sip of coffee. "It's a nice nod to the holiday theme."

Melinda blew out a breath. "Good."

"You constructed a fabulous scavenger hunt, Melinda." Reaching across the table, he took the hand resting there. "I definitely hope next year everyone has a chance to follow the clues."

"I hope so, too." She linked her fingers with his. "I'm glad you've had a chance to experience all Holly Pointe has to offer."

"I enjoyed the activities and the town, but the best part has been you." His fingers tightened on hers. "I know people talk about holiday romances, but that's not how I see what we're building. I care about you, Melinda. I know things have moved quickly, but that's—"

"Jack."

He turned toward the feminine voice. His eyes lit with recognition at the sight of the petite brunette. Pushing back his chair, Jack stood and extended both hands to the woman. "Lara, this is a surprise. It's good to see you."

Lara squeezed his hands, then stepped back and gestured to the man at her side. "Jack, this is Steve Freier with Classic DineCo. Steve, Jack McPherson with the Timberhaven Group."

Jack turned to the man with the stylishly cut silver hair.

"It's nice to put a face with a name. I've heard good things about your company." Jack slanted a quick glance at Lara before returning his attention to Steve. "You buy up historic buildings and convert them into bars and restaurants."

"We do."

Steve might have an easy manner, Melinda thought, but he had sharp eyes. Eyes that now scanned the diner.

Melinda slowly rose to her feet.

"I don't believe I've met either of you." Melinda stepped forward, offered a friendly smile and extended her hand. "I'm Melinda Kelly."

Both shook her hand, and Lara became all smiles. "You're Rosie's daughter."

"I am."

"Your mother told us all about you." Lara's voice was as warm as her brown eyes.

"Well, then, you have the advantage." Melinda kept the smile on her face and gestured to the two empty chairs at the table. "Please, join us."

Glancing at Steve, Lara got a slight nod. "We'd love to, but we can't stay long. Rosie should be right—"

"I'm here." Rosie practically sang the words as she rushed over. "I'm sorry I was delayed. I got to talking to some friends outside." Rosie looked at Melinda. "I see you've met Steve and Lara."

"We just finished the introductions," Melinda said.

"I'm sure Jack didn't need any." Rosie flashed him a brilliant smile. "He's the one who put Lara and me in touch."

Melinda turned to Jack. "Is that so?"

Her mother didn't wait for Jack to respond. "Yes, he gave her my contact information. Lara and I have had several lovely conversations." Rosie smiled at Lara. "We hit it off right away."

"Your mom was so charming on the phone that she persuaded me to come and see the place for myself. I'd given her numerous possibilities, but then I thought about adding Steve and his group to the mix." Lara smiled at Steve. "I had a feeling this café would be perfect for DineCo, so I convinced Steve to come with me."

Somehow Melinda managed to keep a smile on her face as she turned to her mother. "You're considering selling?"

Rosie gave a noncommittal shrug. "All options are on the table."

"Well, then I'm sure the three of you have a lot to discuss." With great effort, Melinda kept her voice even. "Jack and I were ready to leave, but I can stay and listen in if you'd like—"

"Oh, no, honey." Rosie put a hand on Melinda's arms. "Thank you, but not necessary. You enjoy this time with Jack."

On the way out of the café, Melinda's heart pounded so hard she could barely hear herself think. She clasped her hands together to still their trembling.

By the time she reached Jack's car and slid into the passenger seat, the chill in the outside air was no match for the chill that had taken up residence in her heart.

She didn't bother buckling her seat belt.

Jack didn't bother starting the car.

"Why is this the first I'm hearing about this consultant?" she asked.

"The first time I ate at the diner, your mother asked me if I knew any restaurant consultants. I told her I did and would give Lara her contact information. After that, it was up to them."

Her gaze remained focused on his face. "What about Steve?"

"Lara does some work for my group, but she has other clients. Classic DineCo must be a new one," Jack mused, his brows knit together. "I had no idea she would pull them in." Jack's gaze searched her face. "Melinda, based on everything you said about your mom talking of change but never acting on it, I honestly didn't expect it to go any further."

"So, you remember me saying that, but you don't remember

192 | CINDY KIRK

me saying how these big corporations moving into Holly Pointe just to capitalize on tourists are hurting our community?" Melinda pressed her eyes shut and shook her head. She had read the interest all over Steve's face. And Jack was a businessman—there's no way he hadn't seen it, too, couldn't have known the potential outcomes of his actions. "My mom could end up selling the diner."

Jack spoke gently "Would that really be so bad? You said you didn't want to run the diner. She's clearly making plans with Carl—"

"This is not about my mother and Carl! Don't try and change the subject." Melinda couldn't believe what Jack was saying. Maybe she didn't want to personally run the diner, but everything inside her wept at the thought of Rosie's Diner falling into uncaring hands.

On Christmas Eve, when Derek had mentioned them filling the salt and pepper shakers, the memory of those happy times had wrapped around her heart. Sure, her mother had worked a lot, but the diner had been their second home and the staff and the customers their extended family. Did Jack really think it was just a business to her? That she wouldn't care about him helping to dismantle it?

"It's not about me wanting to manage the diner." Melinda blew out a breath. "It's bigger. Rosie's Diner is part of the fabric of the community. It's a vibrant part of the Holly Pointe community."

She thought about Sugarplum's and Jingle Shells with their out-of-state owners.

"We live here. We sponsor local events. We're invested in Holly Pointe and what happens here in a way that a distant, corporate owner could never be."

He remained silent for several seconds.

"You don't see it, do you?"

"I'm sorry, Melinda." His voice softened. "I see now that you're more emotionally involved and invested in the diner than I realized."

"It's doesn't matter."

"It does matter." Jack reached over as if to take her hand, but she pulled back. "Listen to me, Melinda. I legitimately thought I was helping. You wanted your mom to make changes. Lara was a resource, a tool to help her make those changes."

"A resource who brought in someone who's interested in buying the diner." Melinda took a calming breath, but found it didn't work. "Rosie's Diner is my mom's life, and now I'm afraid she's going to sell it off."

Melinda glanced out the passenger side window. When she turned back, she was overcome with an incredible sadness. No matter how close she felt to Jack, no matter how wonderful the past few days had been, it was just that—only a few days.

"You don't understand me, what I care about. You don't have the same vision for the future that I do."

"That's not true. I miscalculated, Melinda, that's all. It doesn't mean I don't recognize what matters to you—"

"Yes, it does." Melinda fought to keep her voice level. "That's exactly what it means. These last few days...it's all been so..." *Magical, romantic, perfect.* The list running through her head didn't bring her comfort. "It's all been so fast that we're not seeing what's real, that we are still basically strangers to each other." Melinda stared down at her hands, too unsure of her emotions to risk looking at Jack.

For a few moments, they sat in silence. Then Jack spoke.

"Maybe you're right." His gaze locked on some distant spot beyond the windshield. "Maybe we don't really see each other."

As it seemed there was nothing further to say, he started the car and drove her home. He came inside and slowly gathered his things.

Melinda had the feeling he was waiting for her to ask him to sit and talk this out.

She didn't.

She'd thought he understood what was important to her. Heck, deep down, she'd thought she might have at long last found her soul mate.

No, there was nothing more to say.

She let him walk out the door.

Melinda didn't contact her mother until the next day when word reached her that Lara and Steve had left town. The two hadn't stayed long, barely twenty-four hours. Melinda wasn't sure if that was a good sign or not.

She texted her mother and asked if she could stop over that evening. Melinda forgot to say she preferred it just be the two of them. On the drive over, she worried Carl might be hanging around. But when she pulled into her mother's driveway, his vehicle was nowhere in sight.

Rosie met her at the door, stepping aside to let her enter.

"Thanks for meeting with me."

"If you hadn't texted, I'd have called you."

Slipping off her coat, Melinda hung it up, then turned. "To tell me your big news?"

Puzzlement furrowed Rosie's brow. "What big news?"

"That you're selling the diner."

"Oh, Melinda." Rosie shook her head. "You really are making a mess of things."

"Me?" Melinda's voice rose. "What are you talking about? I'm not the one selling the diner."

"Forget the diner for now. I'm talking about you making a mess of things with Jack. Who, by the way, was only doing what I asked him to do when he put me in touch with Lara."

Caught off-balance by the abrupt change in subject, Melinda blinked. "How did you—"

"He called me to apologize for any problems he caused between us. I refrained from telling him that he wasn't the problem, *you* are. But I'm not inclined to hold back with you."

Melinda ignored her mother's chastisement, a tactic she'd been perfecting since junior high. "I would have never brought Jack to Holly Pointe if I'd known he was going to pressure you to sell."

"Oh please, Melinda. When have you ever known anyone to pressure me into doing anything?" Stepping into the living room, Rosie motioned for Melinda to follow.

When her mother pointed to a chair, Melinda sat, and Rosie took the one beside her.

"I simply asked Jack if he knew anyone in the restaurant business who could give me some advice. What would you have expected him to do? Lie to me? Not offer help? Does that sound like the man you know?" Rosie's lips suddenly curved. "Lara is a lovely woman. We hit it off right away. Though, her bringing Steve here was a surprise."

"I don't understand why you thought you needed outside advice in the first place. I've been giving you suggestions for years, and you haven't tried any of them. Is it that you don't think I know what I'm doing?"

"Honey, this has nothing to do with me not valuing your input. It has to do with the fact that this is not your dream. Running a café has never been your dream. You need to live your own life and go after what you want. You let me worry about my business."

"But I want to help you."

Rosie continued as if Melinda hadn't spoken. "If Rosie's Diner is going to not only survive, but thrive, I believe an in-depth analysis needs to be done on all aspects of the business. Just the analysis will cost big bucks. Selling may end up being the best option."

Melinda inhaled sharply.

Reaching over, Rosie laid a comforting hand on her daughter's arm. "For the record, I'm not ready to throw in the towel. Not yet, anyway. But it's good to know that buyers are out there in case that changes."

"Selling is up to you." Melinda forced out the words.

"You're right, it is up to me. Which is why, instead of worrying about my business, you should be worrying about your own."

"My own what?"

"Your business with Jack." Rosie's gaze turned serious. "Instead of sitting here talking with me, you should be home packing for your trip to Mexico."

"How do you know about Mexico?"

"Jack mentioned it to Carl." Rosie smiled. "Carl tells me everything."

"Who's going to Mexico?" Derek strolled into the room.

Melinda turned to her brother. "I didn't know you were here."

"I came in the back." Derek gestured to the kitchen. "Mom texted she had leftovers for Cam and me."

Rosie stood. "I'd love to stay and chat with you two, but I'm meeting Carl. If you and Jack want any of the leftovers, you can work that out with Derek."

Her and Jack? Didn't her mother understand there was no more *her and Jack*?

Rosie pulled on her coat, grabbed her car keys and was out the door before Derek turned back to Melinda. "So you and Jack are finally going to make it to Mexico. Good for you."

"That was the plan." Melinda blew out a breath. "Jack and I, well, we've had what you might call a falling out."

"Falling out? Seriously?" Derek grinned. "I haven't heard that term since Great-Grandma was around."

Melinda glared. "You know what I mean."

"You had a fight." Derek dropped down onto the love seat. "It happens. Big deal. There's still time."

"Time for what?"

"To make things right."

The yearning that rose up inside Melinda was so strong it brought tears to her eyes. She hurriedly blinked back the moisture.

"It's not that simple. You'd never understand anyway." Melinda fought against envy. "Things are so easy between you and Shiloh."

Derek snorted.

"What? Are you having problems?"

Derek rolled his eyes. "No, Melinda, no problems. But 'easy' is a stretch. The attraction was easy, sure. I knew I was attracted to Shiloh right when I met her. One date with her and I was hooked. But just because the beginning was easy doesn't mean the rest always will be. We're human. We make mistakes. We disagree. We get past it."

"No parts of relationships have ever been easy for me. Not the beginnings, definitely not the ends."

"Because you hadn't met the right guy."

"I was with Alex for almost three years," she reminded her brother.

"So what? Time isn't what makes someone right for you. Alex wasn't your person." Derek's tone turned matter-of-fact. "Don't get me wrong, Alex was a nice guy—he just wasn't your person."

"Is Shiloh your person?"

"Honestly, I don't know."

"Why? You seem so happy. And you just said there were no problems." Melinda gazed at Derek in disbelief. "I thought you loved her."

"Melinda, it's not problems versus perfection. Look, I really like Shiloh, but I'm not sure I love her. And I'm almost certain she has the same doubts." Derek sat forward, resting his forearms on his thighs. "Shiloh has dreams, big dreams. She wants to go on tour with her band and make a career with her music. That kind of life doesn't appeal to me. Could that change down the road?" Derek shrugged. "Maybe? Too soon to know."

"What about Camryn? She adores Shiloh."

"Cam will be fine. I let her know that while I care about Shiloh, nothing is certain. Plus, she's old enough to know that not every woman I date is auditioning to be her mom."

Melinda recalled how Shiloh's eyes lit up whenever Derek walked into the room. "Aren't you worried Shiloh will be heart-broken if you break up?"

"Isn't having your heart broken always a risk when you're in a relationship? I would never intentionally do anything to be cruel to or to hurt Shiloh, but I also won't stay in a relationship that doesn't work just to spare someone's feelings."

Melinda brought a hand to her head as if that would bring her spinning thoughts under control. "Have you ever thought this whole bit about you and Shiloh not wanting the same things might just be an excuse? Do you ever worry that you can't love someone after Camryn's mom?"

"Absolutely not." Derek's tone was firm. "I understand it's easy to feel that way when you see all your friends coupled up and you're still looking for your person. But not having found the right person doesn't mean that something is wrong, it's just timing. The way I see it, the right person comes along when they're meant to. In the meantime, until the right woman comes along, I'll just keep enjoying the wrong ones."

Melinda could only shake her head. He made it sound so easy.

"Enough talk." Derek jumped up from the sofa. "I need to grab those leftovers and get home."

"I'll help you." Melinda rose and followed her brother into the kitchen.

Derek's words circled around and around in her head the rest of the evening.

It's not problems versus perfection.

Time isn't what makes someone right for you.

Just because the beginning was easy doesn't mean the rest always will be.

There's still time to make things right.

CHAPTER TWENTY-ONE

On Thursday morning, Jack heaved his suitcase into the trunk of his rental car and slammed the lid shut. He was nearly to the cabin door when he heard a truck approaching. When the vehicle came into view, Jack steeled himself for what was coming.

Pulling his truck to a stop behind Jack's car, Derek jumped out. He covered the short distance between them in several long strides.

"Look." Jack held up a hand. "I'm sure you're as upset as Melinda—"

A startled look crossed Derek's face, then he laughed. "Gimme a break."

"You're not upset?"

"Over my mom and those consultants?"

Jack nodded.

"Not at all. Rose Kelly does what she wants. Always has, always will." Derek clapped Jack on the back. "I've no beef with you. My sister might be upset with you, but we're solid. I personally believe it's good for my mom to explore all options."

"Melinda doesn't see it that way." Everything inside Jack clenched tight. He wasn't angry with Melinda. He was disappointed with himself. How could he have read the signs so wrong? "I messed things up with her, Derek. I thought I knew what she wanted."

"My sister barely knows what she wants. If she hasn't figured herself out in thirty years, how could you be expected to in a matter of days?" Derek glanced at the cabin door. "You have a Coke or something to drink in there?"

Jack blinked. "You want a soda?"

"Naw, I was just asking to see if you had one." Derek chuckled. "Yeah, I want a soda."

"I have several. I was going to leave them behind for the cleaning crew." Jack strode into the cabin with Derek behind him.

In minutes, they were seated with bottles of Coke in hand and a bowl of chips in the middle of the table.

"I'm not trying to drag on my sister. What I was trying to say outside is that Mel worries a lot." Derek bit into a chip and followed it with a swig of Coke. "Bottom line, you make her happy. If you didn't exactly know what she needed or wanted or whatever, so what? None of us are mind readers."

Jack nodded.

"The fact that you're worried about her feelings tells me you care." Derek leaned back in the wooden chair. "Just relax and give it time. You two will figure it out."

"Melinda wants nothing to do with me." Jack raked a hand through his hair. "Not surprising, really. I'm notoriously bad with women. I have a head for business. I do not have a head for women."

"Join the club." Derek laughed, but quickly sobered. "My sister likes you. You like her. I don't have a vote, but if I did, I'd say give yourselves another chance."

Jack pushed to his feet, knowing the next move was Melinda's. He only wished he knew if she was willing to give him—give them—another chance. "I need to get on the road."

"You're leaving?" Surprise skittered across Derek's face. "Now?"

Jack nodded. "I texted Melinda earlier to say I still want to go to Mexico with her. Our rebooked flight leaves at noon tomorrow. She didn't respond, but if she changes her mind, I'll be on that flight."

~

Derek was finishing off his second Coke and the rest of the chips while contemplating just how messy relationships could be when he heard a car drive up. Seconds later, a knock sounded at the door.

Cleaning crew, he thought, popping another chip into his mouth.

Another knock, more insistent this time.

Surely Kate had given them a key?

The next knock, harder than the first two, rattled the doorframe.

Derek reached the front door just as it was shoved open. He jumped back.

"Hey," he protested. "Watch it. You nearly hit me in the nose."

"I'm sorry. I knocked." His sister stepped into the cabin and scanned the room. "Where's Jack?"

"Gone."

Melinda inhaled sharply. "Gone where?"

"Back to New York."

Expelling a shaky breath, Melinda collapsed into a nearby chair. "I waited too long."

Derek studied her stricken face. "I think Jack's afraid he's blown it with you."

"I'm the one who blew it." Melinda gazed at him, her expression bleak. "I was falling in love with him, and now he's gone. I don't know what to do, Derek."

Derek wondered just when he'd been elevated to the role of relationship counselor.

"Well, the bad news is he's already left. The good news is I have time to drive you to the airport." Even as he spoke, Derek wondered if Melinda would be bold enough to shove aside her fears and take that step. "Your flight to Mexico leaves tomorrow at noon. If you want to salvage your relationship with Jack, I suggest you be on that plane."

∾

Melinda gave her brother a fierce hug before she got out of his truck curbside at JFK. "Safe trip back, and thanks."

"Since I'm here, I'm going to drop off our gifts to Faith and Graham." Derek's tone remained upbeat, but Melinda saw the worry in his eyes. "I'll be in the city for a couple of hours at least."

Without her brother saying the words, Melinda knew what he was telling her. If things didn't go well with Jack and she ended up not getting on the plane, he would be around to take her back to Holly Pointe.

"It's all good." Did speaking confidently, saying the words aloud, make it so? Melinda hoped it did. Yet, she'd hedged her bets, too.

Instead of checking a bag, she'd stuffed everything into a carry-on, figuring she could buy whatever else she needed in Mexico.

If, somehow, she didn't end up getting on the plane, her bag containing her clothing and personal items would remain with her instead of winging its way to Mexico without her.

"This isn't a parking zone," a uniformed officer called out. "Move it."

Mouthing "good-bye" to her brother, Melinda shut the door and picked up her bag.

Because she was running late, once inside the terminal, she

focused on making it to the gate for her flight, weaving through travelers who walked as if they were on a Sunday stroll.

Though she and Derek had allowed enough time to get to the airport, an accident on the highway had tossed the thought of a leisurely drive out the window. There had been a moment or two when she'd wondered if she'd even make it to the airport before the plane took off.

You made it this far, she reassured herself. Now it was time to take the next step.

Lani and Bill had said one of their secrets to a happy marriage was a willingness to admit when you're wrong. Melinda knew she could have called or texted Jack to let him know she was sorry, but she wanted to apologize in person.

The sight of the gate had her quickening her pace. Last she'd checked, the flight was on time. Now, it was boarding.

Melinda scanned the crowd. She turned to a young woman whose spiky dark hair sported platinum tips. "What groups have boarded so far?"

The woman looked up from her phone. "First class and those with kids or needing extra help."

Most of those boarding now appeared to be singles or couples. Her heart began to beat an erratic rhythm as she scanned the group for a second time.

Could Jack have gotten an upgrade and already be on board? If that had happened, it meant he'd given up on her, on them.

Pressing her back against one of the columns, Melinda fought to keep the tears pressing against the backs of her lids from falling.

She tried to tell herself he wasn't her person, but in her heart, she knew he could be.

"Melinda."

She whirled, and there he was—her person, her Jack.

Relief washed across his handsome face. "I wasn't sure you'd come."

"I wasn't sure you'd want me to come." Melinda offered a tremulous smile. "But I hoped."

"I hoped, too."

For several seconds, they simply stared at each other. Melinda caught the young woman giving them the side-eye, but paid her no mind.

"I'm sorry. For everything." Melinda met his blue eyes firmly. "I have no excuse."

"I should have let you know I'd given Lara your mom's contact information. I—"

Melinda waved that away, shaking her head. "I overreacted. I didn't realize myself just how much the diner means to me until that point. I came to your cabin to tell you that, and apologize, but you were already gone."

"The important thing is you're here now." He took her arm. "I bet one day, we'll look back on this time and laugh."

"I'm not so sure about that." Still, she couldn't stop the grin.

Part of it was relief that he was here, that he'd waited for her. Part of it was the belief that he was her person and they'd been given a second chance.

Melinda filled him in on the harrowing drive to the airport and her fear she wouldn't make it in time. He told her he'd spent yesterday tying up loose ends at work.

"As soon as I returned to the city, I met with my team and finished up several pending work items. I wanted to be able to totally relax on this trip with you."

Her gaze met his, and the smiles they exchanged were filled with promise.

"This is the final boarding call for passengers Kelly and McPherson booked on Flight 1327 to Cancun. The final checks are being completed, and the captain will order the doors of the aircraft to close in approximately five minutes. I repeat, this is the final boarding call for passengers Kelly and McPherson. Thank you."

Looking around, Melinda realized that, other than employees, they were the only ones at the gate. She gestured toward the door leading to the jetway. "I guess we better get on the plane."

"I guess we better." Smiling, Jack took her bag, adding it the one slung over his shoulder, the same leather duffel he'd had the day they first met.

Only when she stepped onto the plane and the flight attendant directed her to her seat did Melinda discover her ticket had been upgraded to first class.

"This is going to be so much fun." She slipped into her wide leather seat by the window and fastened her seat belt, eager to get this adventure started.

Jack settled into the seat beside her. After fastening his seat belt, he leaned over and kissed her, long and slow and sweet.

Melinda wasn't sure what to think when a hand came from behind to tap her shoulder.

She turned, and there were Lani and Bill, sitting behind them, broad smiles on their faces.

"Hey, you guys." Melinda smiled and shook her head. "What are the odds?"

"I told Bill on the way here, 'Wouldn't it be fun if you two were on the same flight?'" Lani chattered, gesturing wildly with her hands. "Now, here you are. It's like fate or magic or something."

Fate. Magic. Or simply a new beginning heralded by a Christmas Moon.

Whatever it was, Melinda was buckled in and ready for a wild ride.

I'm ho-ho-hoping that reading Jack and Melinda's love story brought much holiday sparkle into your life.

Each book in the Holly Pointe series can be read as a stand-alone, but most readers find that once they read one, they want to read them all!

These uplifting and charming holiday stories set in gorgeous Holly Pointe, Vermont are a joy to write and I hope they bring the spirit of warmth and kindness into your home and heart.

In Christmas Moon Over Holly Pointe, you saw Dustin and Krista and their two adorable twin boys.

If you'd like to see how their love story began—and see more of other favorite characters—grab your copy of HOME FOR THE HOLLY DAYS, book 1 in the Holly Pointe series.

Or, continue reading for a sneak peek:

SNEAK PEEK OF HOME FOR THE HOLLY DAYS

Chapter One

Krista Ankrom gazed out the restaurant's ninth-floor window at the festive scene below. The Norway spruce decorated for Christmas stood tall and majestic in Rockefeller Center. The splendor of its 50,000 LED lights was surpassed only by the Swarovski star at the top. Krista remembered a news anchor mentioning yesterday at the tree lighting that the star was covered with three million crystals.

The gorgeous scene should have buoyed her flagging spirits, as should this impromptu lunch with her friend.

Across the table, Desz Presley answered work emails and sipped her drink. It was a given that when she and Desz visited L'Avenue for lunch, her friend would multitask while enjoying sea bass and an Aperol Spritz.

Krista returned her attention to the tree covered in multicolored lights, the throngs of tourists skating in front of it, and the Salvation Army Santa on the corner. An engaging scene straight out of a Hallmark movie. Most years, she lovingly drank it in.

"Krista? Are you listening?"

"Hmmm? What? Sorry, Desz. I spaced out watching the skaters." Krista waved an airy hand, not wanting to burden her friend with her thoughts.

"What, you mean you weren't riveted by me complaining about my parents again?"

Though Desz had fully embraced life in NYC since moving here three years ago, at Christmas she loved going home to Tennessee and her family's lavish Christmas celebrations. This year, Desz's parents had opted for a cruise, leaving Desz to spend Christmas in the city.

"I know how you feel." Krista pulled her gaze from the window to give her friend her full attention. "I hoped my family would come spend Christmas with me this year. But Tom and his wife just had their first child, and traveling with a baby can be difficult."

Desz took another sip of her drink. "Remind me why you aren't going there?"

"I considered it until I learned Claire's parents are also spending the holidays with them. It'll be a full house." Krista lifted her glass of spring water. "It figures the one year I'm free, enjoying a family Christmas isn't an option."

"You've always worked over the holidays." Desz sipped her drink, a thoughtful look creasing her brow. "Or you have every year since we first met."

"I planned to get the Japan job and be in Tokyo this month. Not meant to be." Krista had known the repeatedly delayed contract offer had been a bad sign. It didn't matter what her agent, Merline, said about age being no cause for concern, at twenty-eight, Krista understood the realities of her situation.

She'd been right to be concerned. The model chosen to be the new face of Shibusa Cosmetics was a decade younger than she was.

"You'll get another account. A bigger, better one." Desz's voice rang with confidence. "Shibusa will regret not choosing you."

Krista lifted her water in a toast. "I'll drink to that."

Her mocking tone had Desz chuckling before she changed the subject. "At least your parents are staying home to spend Christmas with their first grandchild. My parents are choosing a seafood buffet on the lido deck over me. In what world is that tradition?"

Krista laughed. "No more than working over the holidays can be considered a tradition."

"I'd say you're due for a change." Desz's dark eyes sparkled. "You're an independent woman with enough money to do whatever you want. You should go somewhere. Hey, what am I saying? *We* should go somewhere. Where do you want to go? Totally your call."

An image of the quaint community she'd loved near the Canadian border flashed in Krista's mind. "It's not a place you'd be interested in."

Desz leaned forward. "You let me decide."

"Holly Pointe." Simply saying the name brought a smile to Krista's lips. "Before I got my first big modeling contract and moved to New York, my family spent every Christmas in Vermont."

"Holly Pointe, Vermont." Desz rolled the name around on her tongue, then smiled. "I've never been that far north."

"It's lovely there." Krista sighed. "A picture postcard of how life can be."

Desz cocked her head. "Huh?"

"People in Holly Pointe care about one another. Everyone takes time to enjoy the holidays." Krista smiled, remembering all the events. "There's always a big tree lighting, followed by caroling in the town square. Santa is, well, everywhere. All the buildings are decorated and—"

Krista stopped herself, recalling the elaborate traditions Desz had told her about in Nashville. "It's very humble compared to the Christmas celebrations you're used to."

"It sounds fabulous." Desz clasped her hands together. "I've never experienced a small-town Christmas."

It almost sounded as if Desz was open to going to Holly Pointe. Krista's smile grew. If she couldn't be with her family at Christmas, maybe being in a place that reminded her of them would be the next best thing.

"Does going there for several weeks sound like something you'd want to do?" Krista knew Desz could work from anywhere, and a few weeks someplace free of billboards and ad agencies might help her stop stressing about work.

"I can be packed and ready to leave tomorrow morning."

For the first time since learning she hadn't gotten the Shibusa account, Krista experienced a surge of holiday happiness. She lifted her glass. "To the best Christmas ever."

Desz clinked her glass against Krista's. "To new adventures."

Dustin Bellamy strode down Fifth Avenue, a man on a mission. Out of the corner of his eye, he saw a guy burst out of a store and barrel his way toward the curb where a cab had just pulled up.

The man brushed past him, would have clipped him, if Dustin's reflexes hadn't been good. Built like a bull, the guy reminded Dustin of Stan, a teammate. Stan with his hard wrist shot and a willingness to drop the gloves.

God, he missed his friends. Even the hot-tempered ones.

Lost in thought for several seconds, Dustin stood there while the crowd parted around him. Then he began walking, not wanting to keep the doctor waiting. Though Dustin had to sprint the last two blocks, he stepped off the elevator on the fifth floor with three minutes to spare.

The receptionist, an attractive woman with blonde hair, stood when Dustin entered.

"I'm Dustin Bellamy," he told her. "I have an appointment with Dr. Wallace."

"I know who you are," she said with a smile. "Let me show you the way."

Instead of an exam room, she ushered him into the doctor's luxurious private office.

She inclined her head. "May I get you something to drink while you wait?"

Dustin shook his head. "I'm fine. Thanks."

"The doctor should only be a few minutes." With the promise hanging in the air, she pulled the door closed behind her.

Restless, Dustin wandered the spacious area with its huge flat-screen TV and a standing desk in walnut. A wall of shelves near a sitting area held not only books, but medical awards and several modern sculptures of athletes.

Eric Wallace, orthopedic surgeon and sports medicine guru, had come highly recommended. Though only in his late forties, he was the team physician for several professional sports teams as well as numerous top athletes.

Dustin moved to the window and glanced down on the busy street below. He turned when he heard the door open, his heart kicking into high gear.

Tall and lean, the doctor moved with the grace of an athlete, holding out a hand as he crossed the last few feet to Dustin.

"Eric Wallace. It's a pleasure to finally meet you, Mr. Bellamy." His hand closed around Dustin's in a firm shake. "I'm a huge fan. Please, have a seat."

The doctor gestured to an area with several chairs and a small sofa. Dustin chose one, and the doctor sat in another opposite his.

After a few minutes of polite conversation, Dr. Wallace got down to business. "I reviewed your records and the most recent MRI. You're aware that normally the ACL tears when the muscles around the knee are weak. Because of all the skating you do, that isn't the case with you, not in regard to your previous injury or with this most recent one. Your tests show the muscles around your knee are well-developed and strong. But hockey puts a lot of stress on the ligament due to the twisting, pivoting and cutting."

"The original tear was from a collision with another player," Dustin offered, though the information was in the records.

Wallace nodded. "After the first injury, it appears you had excellent surgical results from the tendon graft."

"I worked hard at rehab." Dustin kept his attention on the doctor's face, searching for the slightest hint of encouragement. "After seven months of intense work, I was back to a hundred percent when I returned to the ice."

The doctor nodded, his expression softening. "I watched the game where you were checked. You kept playing despite reinjuring the ligament."

"It was the first game of the finals." Dustin lifted his chin to meet the doctor's questioning gaze head on. "The trainers braced the knee."

"I'm sure you were aware that playing with a damaged ACL opened you up to further injury." The doctor spoke in a matter-of-fact tone.

"My team needed me. We were in the playoffs." Dustin's breathing wanted to spike, but he kept it slow and easy. "I have no regrets. Winning the Cup was worth it. Since June, I've worked on staying fit and healthy. I can skate, but it's clear that without surgery I won't be able to get back to a competitive level."

Dr. Wallace sat back in his chair, regret blanketing his face. "I'm sorry, Dustin. I can't recommend another surgery."

"I don't think you understand. I'm willing—eager—to do whatever it takes." Dustin leaned forward. "What about platelet-rich plasma treatments to speed healing? I know you've used it on hockey players."

"PRP treatments can speed healing and stimulate tissue regeneration in the treated area after surgery. However, as I stated, I can't recommend a second ACL surgical intervention for you." Compassion filled the doctor's blue eyes. "Not based on the extent of your injury."

Dustin had to stop himself from jumping up and railing at the doctor. Didn't the man understand? Hockey was more than a game to him. It was his life.

Over the years, Dustin had become an expert at pushing past the pain. Most of the time, it was physical. Hockey—at any level, but especially at the highest level—was hard on the body. It also demanded a mental toughness.

Cultivating that toughness paid off now as he kept his expression impassive, showing no reaction to the news.

"I realize this isn't what you hoped to hear." The doctor's voice gentled. "I concur with your team specialist and the other physician you saw that the second injury to your ACL and playing while injured contributed to what we're seeing on the MRI. Surgery is not advised and, if done, would not give you the desired results."

Dustin had heard it all before. Still, he'd held out hope.

"Is there a chance you're wrong?" Dustin had never been one to give up easily. That tenacity and determination had served him well over the years. "Like I said, I'm willing to put in the work, do whatever—"

"I'm not wrong." Despite the firm tone, sympathy filled the doctor's pale blue eyes. "The fact that you've worked so hard on your rehab after the first surgery is why you were able to go back. Continuing to play after sustaining the second injury was a game changer."

As much as he wanted to return to his team, Dustin wouldn't go back and be less. His teammates, who wanted to win, deserved better.

Pushing to his feet, Dustin stuck out his hand. "I appreciate your time."

The doctor rose and gave his hand a firm shake. "You were an amazing player."

Were. Even the doctor was speaking in the past tense.

Dustin rode the elevator down to the main floor of the midtown office building, disappointment and grief battering at his control.

Helping his team win the Stanley Cup had been worth it, he reminded himself. Despite the positive thoughts, when he stepped outside, Dustin had to stop to catch his breath.

Hockey had been his life. The other players, his family. All that was gone now.

The irritating buzz of his phone had him setting his jaw in a hard line. If some reporter had gotten his private number…

Dustin jerked the phone from his pocket and glanced at the display. He took a steadying breath before he answered. "Hi, Dad."

"How did the doctor's visit go?" The carefully cultivated easy tone didn't fool Dustin. His father was as apprehensive about this visit as he'd been.

"Wallace concurs with the other two."

Silence for one, two, three long seconds.

"Perhaps there's someone else. I heard of a doctor in—"

"Dad. This guy was thorough." Dustin kept his tone matter-of-fact, understanding this news was nearly as devastating to his father as it was to him.

Hockey hadn't just been Dustin's life for the past twenty-plus years, starting with peewee leagues, it had been his father's life, as well.

"I'm sorry, son." Terry Bellamy cleared his throat, then spoke in a light tone. "What are you going to do? You are the Player with the Plan, after all."

The moniker the media had given Dustin early in his career

had stuck. He'd not only been a physical player, but he'd managed his emotions and kept his focus. He'd played smart. Not only on the ice, but in how he'd managed his career.

The six-year multimillion-dollar contract he'd signed shortly before his first injury had been one of the smartest.

"I'm considering several possibilities. Freddie and I will be discussing all my options in more depth."

His dad didn't push. From the time he'd been drafted at twenty-two, Dustin had been in charge of his career. With, of course, input from his agent, Freddie Wurtz.

"Your mom and I would love to have you home this Christmas."

"I have no doubt Ashleigh's boys will keep you both extremely busy." Dustin's sister had four kids under eight. His mom and dad doted on their grandsons.

"They'd love to see Uncle Dustin." His dad's tone turned persuasive. He obviously was not ready to give up without a fight.

Dustin had no doubt some of his tenacity came from this man, who'd been such a strong support all these years.

Which was why Dustin knew he needed a good reason not to go to Minnesota and spend Christmas with the family. Not wanting to deal with questions about his future wouldn't be considered an acceptable excuse.

"There's this woman I've been seeing." Dustin kept his tone casual. "I'm going to spend the holidays with her."

"Oh. Really?" His dad's voice held surprise. "You haven't mentioned anyone. You always said hockey and relationships are impossible together."

"That's what I thought." Dustin hadn't mentioned anyone, because there was no one to mention. But he couldn't deal with the family right now, so fictional girlfriend it was. "Thanks for all you've done, Dad. I couldn't have made it this far without you."

"You sound as if your life is over." Worry filled his dad's voice. "This is simply the beginning of a new chapter."

"It is." Dustin spoke with more confidence than he felt at the moment. "We'll talk later."

No longer the Player with the Plan, Dustin began walking and soon found himself at Rockefeller Center, gazing down at the skaters going around and around on the ice.

The tree and other signs of the approaching holiday season seemed a mockery of the sadness that held him in a stranglehold.

What am I going to do?

The grip on his chest tightened at the question.

He pulled out his phone, then realized he had no one to call. His best friends were also his teammates, and he wasn't ready to talk to them about this. Regardless of what he'd said to his dad, he also didn't want to deal with his agent. Not yet. And he couldn't call a girlfriend who didn't exist.

In this city of millions, Dustin suddenly felt very alone. His lavish hotel suite held no appeal. Besides, when he'd slipped out of the hotel this morning, he'd noticed a couple of sports reporters in the lobby.

He needed a place to lie low. A place to regroup. Most of all, a place that would give him the time and space necessary to come up with a plan.

This small town is full of big surprises that are both merry and bright. Pick up your copy of HOME FOR THE HOLLY DAYS and let this feel-good holiday romance warm your heart.

ALSO BY CINDY KIRK

Good Hope Series

The Good Hope series is a must-read for those who love stories that
uplift and bring a smile to your face.

GraceTown Series

Enchanting stories that are a perfect mixture of romance, friendship, and
magical moments set in a community known for unexplainable
happenings.

Hazel Green Series

These heartwarming stories, set in the tight-knit community of Hazel
Green, are sure to move you, uplift you, inspire and delight you. Enjoy
uplifting romances that will keep you turning the page!

Holly Pointe Series

Readers say "If you are looking for a festive, romantic read this
Christmas, these are the books for you."

Jackson Hole Series

Heartwarming and uplifting stories set in beautiful Jackson Hole,
Wyoming.

Silver Creek Series

Engaging and heartfelt romances centered around two powerful families
whose fortunes were forged in the Colorado silver mines.

Sweet River Montana Series

A community serving up a slice of small-town Montana life, where helping hands abound and people fall in love in the context of home and family.

Made in the USA
Middletown, DE
17 April 2024

53120917R00132